HERE GOES NOTHING

HERE GOES NOTHING

a novel

EAMON McGRATH

ECW

Purchase the print edition
and receive the eBook free.
For details, go to ecwpress.com/eBook.

Editor for the Press: Michael Holmes/a misFit Book
Cover design: Jessic Albert
 Cover illustration: © Joey Gao/www.joey-gao.com
Author photo: Danny Miles

This is a work of fiction. Names, characters,
places, and incidents either are the product of
the author's imagination or are used fictitiously,
and any resemblance to actual persons, living or
dead, business establishments, events, or locales
is entirely coincidental.

LIBRARY AND ARCHIVES CANADA CATALOGUING
IN PUBLICATION

Title: Here goes nothing : a novel / Eamon
McGrath.

Names: McGrath, Eamon, author.

Identifiers: Canadiana (print) 20200233580
Canadiana (ebook) 20200233610

ISBN 978-1-77041-443-3 (softcover)
ISBN 978-1-77305-625-8 (PDF)
ISBN 978-1-77305-624-1 (EPUB)

Classification: LCC PS8625.G72 H47 2020
DDC C813/.6—dc23

The publication of *Here Goes Nothing* has been generously supported by the Canada Council for the Arts which
last year invested $153 million to bring the arts to Canadians throughout the country and is funded in part by the
Government of Canada. *Nous remercions le Conseil des arts du Canada de son soutien. L'an dernier, le Conseil a investi
153 millions de dollars pour mettre de l'art dans la vie des Canadiennes et des Canadiens de tout le pays. Ce livre est financé
en partie par le gouvernement du Canada.* We acknowledge the support of the Ontario Arts Council (OAC), an
agency of the Government of Ontario, which last year funded 1,737 individual artists and 1,095 organizations in 223
communities across Ontario for a total of $52.1 million. We also acknowledge the contribution of the Government
of Ontario through the Ontario Book Publishing Tax Credit, and through Ontario Creates for the marketing of
this book.

PRINTED AND BOUND IN CANADA

PRINTING: MARQUIS   5 4 3 2 1

*To my father, John McGrath, for first
playing me the Clash and the Replacements,
and to my brother Brendan,
who's ten times the musician that I am.*

FREE GAS

We woke up on a Monday morning in Montreal. Everybody met at the van at ten thirty, after a hard night of partying in Mile End. We were staying at a friend's apartment on Rue Saint Viateur and Avenue du Parc. Our plan was to leave the city as soon as possible, get as far west as we could on a bit more than half a tank, and fill up in Ontario where there were no French cops, just in case. We figured the English police might go easier on us.

In those days, we'd gas-and-go everywhere we could, spending what others would on filling-up on bottles of bottom-shelf alcohol instead. Murky had an extra licence plate, so we'd dart into an alleyway close to a station that was near a highway to switch plates, pull in, pump the gas, drive off, and switch them back in the same alley before hitting the road.

Sometimes, we'd be chased and caught, and we'd just play dumb: "Oh shit, sorry, man, I thought he went in to pay," we'd say, pointing at whoever was in the seat beside. Other times, the clerks would never even know that it had happened, and we'd casually and quietly pull out and be on our way.

After a short drive, we arrived in the capital. It was pouring fucking rain, sheets of it. The gas light was on, so we turned right on a red and pulled into a gas station adjacent the massive, sprawling parking lot of a box store complex on Ottawa's outskirts. Murky found a free pump behind a black sports car and pulled the keys from the ignition.

The gas-up routine was all too familiar. Murky got out of the van, his collar pulled over his neck to hide from the wet and cold, went to the nozzle, and filled the tank. He climbed back into the van, coolly pressed his foot down on the gas, and with a "here we go" drove slowly through the empty parking lot of Canadian Tire.

After a few seconds, Eoin said, "Holy shit!"

Behind us, the gas station attendant was barrelling through the parking lot, in a full tilt, holding on to his hat as he blazed through the storm.

"*What* the *fuck!*" Murky even hit the brakes for a second, to get a better rear view and give him a minute to catch up, before calmly accelerating. It was like dangling a carrot in front of a mule. We were howling. I was laughing so hard my stomach hurt—this poor, helpless gas attendant rocketing through the lot without a hope in hell of catching up to us. Yet his enthusiasm was visceral. You could see him losing breath, each step coming closer and closer to having to give up his chase, but still so determined. At the time, it was hilarious. Our lungs and ribs ached with laughter.

Murky must've been going about ten clicks when he pulled up to the turnoff to hit the freeway. Then he accelerated, and the uniformed Canadian Tire attendant got smaller and smaller in the downpour behind us, swearing and yelling in the middle of the empty lot.

"Holy fuck, man," Eoin said. "That fucker *loves* his fuckin' job! Workplace loyalty at its finest!"

In our youthful arrogance, there could really be no feeling quite as good. We got such joy out of such immense misfortune. I'll never forget the jubilation we all felt in those moments when we'd fulfill our burning, reckless desire to take the world for all it had. Of course it was cruel; there were four of us and one of him, and we were out of our minds.

We had a superstition at the time that you couldn't clean the van until the tour was over, so by the time we'd crossed the border westward and slingshotted around the Golden Horseshoe towards home, we were up to our necks in an ocean of garbage. In our minds it was the same as shaving a playoff beard. Stained blankets, liquor bottles, half-eaten bags of potato chips, rotten food, filthy clothes, rumpled sleeping bags, and who knows what else forming a cemented, solidified wall around our bodies in their seats. Whenever we'd pull up to a venue, an avalanche of empty beer cans and two-sixes would come rushing out of the shotgun side door as it opened. Chaos in our wake as always.

For this and every cardinal sin we'd commit before, during, or after a show, we'd have that sacred half hour onstage every night to seek forgiveness. Despite the harrowing feeling of guilt deep inside me, for every poor, desperate gas station attendant running horizontal through the rain, I knew that I'd be back in Ottawa, and all those cities that we'd passed through to get there, in no time, with numerous opportunities to be redeemed.

Still, I'd play this scene, and countless others like it, over and over again in my mind throughout the next few years. With determination, and a fear of letting go, things can be forever preserved in memory. The feelings you get when they happen the first time: the first time your teenage lips touch alcohol, that early and initial lust of arrogance, arms raised underage in the burning night, dizzy with vodka and cheap sugary mixer. The same goes for playing shows and going on tour. My first band, when I was so, so young, hitting the stages of my hometown when the clock struck set time and we were swept away in the blur of lights and that out-of-body rush—pure adrenaline and raw emotion: devoid of music industry careerism.

As time went on, show after show, records and shirts got sold by the box-load, Saturday nights became entire tours, and tours got longer as the years went by. Labels came and went, business instincts developed, slightly, rent got paid, and along with all of it came a steady and unhealthy tolerance to alcohol: two beers before a show became a case split three ways that became whiskey shots at load-in, and that young and dizzy nighttime magic became the darkness of a blackout.

One in five shows still returned me to that distant wash of out-of-body psychedelia, but it seemed like a tolerance for playing live had grown as well—no longer the unexplored labyrinthine world it used to be—the magic gradually replaced by a sense of practicality. With every hour spent loading gear in and out of venues or sitting above van wheels as they spun perpetually on the road, the light of the stage became more and more familiar. It eventually got so my whole life was spent searching for those feelings of early shows, of early drunkenness, of early touring, and that search to relocate something long lost starts to consume your soul.

"When you're touring for a living," you tell yourself, "when you're selling enough records to buy a house, when you're selling out rooms across the world, when the struggle is over, that's when that feeling will return."

You tell yourself that every night. In the depths of sleep, when before you used to dream, you now only hope, plan, and remember.

EVERYBODY KNOWS

I opened my eyes on a beach in Costa Vicentina Natural Park after a transatlantic red-eye flight and a four-hour bus ride south from Lisbon. It was a place that seemed to exist on the fringes of reality and the frontiers of identity. You are responsible for your own time: no clocks hang on the walls in the small sandy patio courtyard in the middle of the surf camp dormitories.

If "nowhere" could be defined as being over a few hundred clicks from the sweat and churn of the nearest bustling city, then this camp is in the middle of it. A ten minutes' drive inland, there is no fixed address. No mail comes. The only thing you'll find upon arrival are those aiming to escape the imprisoning banalities of daily living: hippies, poets, punks, surfers, and me. I went there to begin the longest tour of Europe I'd ever done.

I was far from the cold autumn that was beginning to take shape in Canada. Before I left for Europe, Toronto's trees were starting to look bare, the green retreating from their leaves. The day I left, caught within the soon-to-be skeletal remains of the tallest of those trees that stood in the middle of Yarmouth Road, a red balloon beat against branches as it tried to break free in the wind. It was the start of that time of year where the sun is in a constant state of setting.

I had just started playing guitar for Davey Moodey, a well-known veteran in the Canadian music scene who'd written some long-forgotten radio rock hits in the mid-nineties. A few months earlier, he'd put out a call for new players; some rumours circled about why his band had left him, but the most believable story was that the wear and tear of the road had finally got to them.

Davey seemed to always be on the verge of great success, and this time around he enlisted younger musicians to tour with him, people who still had that hunger to make a living touring all year. Being away from home, being broke and cold, and being in an unstable mental state twenty-four hours a day can kill the desire to keep going, so Davey picked from the newest, freshest crop: those of us who seemed to him unweathered and unaffected. We didn't know how much older than us Davey was, exactly, but he was one of those people who had sort of always been around. With "big break" written all over this opportunity, I left the last of some Ontario dates with a punk band I was playing with to fill the role of lead guitar on tour in the band backing Davey Moodey.

I stayed on tour till the very last second before I caught the plane to Lisbon: I was finishing a show, packing up my gear, and heading to Pearson airport when they were all touching down at Heathrow and making the long, two-to-three day drive to southern Portugal, so, lucky for me, I traded the urban hell of European metropolitan traffic for two days on the beach.

The camp dormitories were situated along a hill surrounded by miles of brown grass and swirling blue sky. The site of the bandshell, located a little farther from the dormitories, stood in front of a backdrop of red rocks that became the cliffs that towered over the Atlantic. Austrians, Germans, and the Dutch visit every summer and fall, escaping the madness of Vienna, the rigid vertices of Berlin, and the tourist hell of Amsterdam for an emotional, artistic, and physical peace. For me, this was home as I waited for the band to come and meet me, get in the van, and drive.

A fridge full of Sagres opened every few seconds as the eager hands of surfers cracked bottles and slammed the contents down their throats. Every morning a bus left at around nine fifteen to take a parade of them to the beach with—so they claimed—the best surf in the entire world. It was September, and the waves were high, so high that no tourists could brave them. Only the best and most experienced surfers from the continent had the guts to tackle the rip there, looking over the ocean westward, toes dangling off the edge of Europe.

My skin was constantly sticky with sweat. Bits of sand would fall from my head as I ran my finger through my hair. There was a salty taste in my mouth from the mist that pressed against the rock as the sun hung like a hand grenade in the sky, beating down in a constant heat all day until the temperature plummeted at nightfall. My clothes had the weight of days of sweat soaked into them. Around us there was nothing, only the curve of land, sharply angled towards the overwhelming blueness of the sunlit sky. Compared to the cold of Canada, this was paradise.

"You need a wave with a good peak," explained the camp's owner, Markus. "You can't have something too powerful; it'll just launch you off your board. You want to be able to see a wave from the shore that's not going to break and turn white until it's closer to the sand."

We were standing on a hill overlooking a beach full of surfers who were trying to catch a rip at the perfect time of day, riders leaping up on their boards and bailing in the water after about five metres of riding.

"The best is when you're in what we call the green room." Markus leaned into me, his words made barely audible by the wind on the beach. "That's where the wave barrels over you, and you're trapped inside a moving tunnel of water, almost at the point where it's going to collapse and crush you. But for half a second, everything goes green. Amazing."

I could only imagine the feeling, like standing behind a waterfall and looking out into the world through a wall of liquid glass.

"The first time it happened, I was awestruck," he continued. "I fell off my board, couldn't believe my eyes. For that one second, you just forget what's real. Time seems to last forever, but at the same time, only exists in that one split, green second."

I thought about that: to be caught within a wave, and how it would feel to be inside. The water would barrel over you as you tried to outrun it all the way to shore. It would be the feeling of nature trying to catch you in its claws, gnashing at your heels. But imagine the excitement of being fast enough to get away, while staring through a thick pane of moving, tunnelling water: a big lens full of infinite light.

For musicians, the greenroom is that comforting place behind the stage, where you get to finally be motionless, close your eyes, nurse a beer, eat some food, get lost in thoughts and ready for the show. Our version of that tunnelling wave is the walls that surround us as we wait for our night to begin. Surfers look out into the world through the wave that tumbles over them as they glide towards the shore, and musicians hear the hum of the support band rumbling through the drywall and concrete, sometimes from floors above or below, as they count down the seconds until set time.

Both have their own magical and mythological overtones. Both are very different views, from inside looking out, and both their own forms of solitary and confined meditation at the very moment of artistic release and expression. Rocketing on top of the water, shirtless and sunburned, but barrelling on and refusing to stop until hitting that moment of absolute exhaustion: that's what a musician does on tour. Your surfboard is your van, your ocean is the asphalt, and your green room is the greenroom. Surfers, however, need only their board, and the gargantuan push and pull of the water. When your surfboard is the van, it's also everything that comes with it: thousands of dollars' worth of equipment bouncing around in the back, being chewed to bits by the eternal stretch of highway that unravels like a ribbon in front of you.

"You cannot fight the ocean," Markus said, before grabbing his board and running off towards the waves. "The ocean always wins."

CHICAGO

There were four of us: Eoin Finnegan, who wrote the songs, sang, and played guitar; Murky Harmsworthy on bass; drummer Walter Latkowski; and me, on lead guitar and backup vocals. It was Eoin's band, and he made quite sure you knew it. The songs were his, and he was the first one to tell you. Eoin was the self-proclaimed "artist type." Selfish both by nature and through his alcoholism, he kept neighbours, housemates, and anyone else up all night with long drinking binges that erupted in cranked stereos and loud guitars and constantly spent the grocery money on a fresh two-six of cheap vodka much to the chagrin of his long list of broken-hearted girlfriends. So Murky did everything else: booked the tours, drove the van, designed the posters, settled with promoters, and most of the time loaded the gear while Eoin and Walter got drunk with girls in the alley. Walter was more or less along for the ride behind the drum kit. Despite all this, nobody ever held anything against anybody. We were all in it together, one for all and all for nothing. We were out of our minds: young, full of come, and maladjusted.

Touring in a Ford Windstar, we'd buy a sixty-pounder every night in the US, after crossing the border illegally, and finish it between four people. We'd steal gas to feed our drinking problems. There were nights where we'd play shows to nobody, but we'd play every single one as if it were our dying last and the room was packed. It was a time when all of touring was mysterious to me: when load-ins were new and exciting, when all I wanted to do with my young body was carry an amplifier up a flight of stairs. Every mile on the road was worth twice its weight in gold, and as we'd head south, north, east, or west from a city, the highway would unclamp its huge and gaping jaw, and it felt like I was moving closer and closer towards the meaning of my life.

We were in Illinois, mid-2008. We left Chicago that morning in a whirlwind of fiery mess. Somehow Eoin and I had the van, which was rare: neither of us had a licence. I drove the wrong direction down a one-way towards the address Murky had read over the payphone, and I'd have still blown over from the night before had we been stopped by the cops. We met him and Walter at the front door of the apartment they'd stayed at, and Murky yanked me from the driver's seat as he got in.

Obama fever was at an all-time high, and the back of the Windstar was plastered with bumper stickers that read, "Yes We Can." Every inch of its silver exterior paint contained his face reduced to the red, white, and blue that had made him a poster boy for hope and change. We were a virulent vehicle for democracy, or what we thought it was: our Canadian licence plate shone like a star shooting down the interstate, and we flaunted every drunken minute of it. I couldn't believe my luck. I'd dropped out of university, joined a rowdy, intoxicated crew of lawless lunatics, and hit the road. I felt like a festival.

A McCain supporter rode our tail before passing, and as he did, I pulled down my pants and pressed my ass firmly against the side window. He honked and gave us the finger and we laughed hysterically, and Eoin, riding shotgun that day, spat out the window at him. I stayed like that as we drove alongside him, crouched up with my whole ass exposed to what seemed to me like the entire Republican Party, until Murky floored it and sped off. We kept laughing all the way to Michigan.

They were all older than me, in their mid-twenties while I was eighteen, maybe nineteen at the time. They'd been on the road for a few years before I joined the band, since they'd been my age, and I looked up to them as road-hardened cowboys with no delusions of grandeur or success clouding their view through the windshield. They toured for touring's sake. For them, that was all there was.

It was a day off, and we thought we'd treat ourselves to a lakeshore motel stay in Macatawa, which was right on the highway towards our next shows in Lansing, Sarnia, and London, en route to what always seemed like the final, climactic destination: Toronto.

That night, Murky got absolutely shitfaced and stormed out of the motel room. I found him shirtless on the beach, waist-deep and yelling in a fever pitch into the filthy, brown water of the undercurrent. Barefoot, I chased after him. He howled into the darkness, dim lights flashing in the distance across the water. Murky hollered and hollered, lifted a gin bottle to his mouth, and took a lengthy swig. He threw the empty into the lake and started walking towards the ravenous waves.

"Murky!" I yelled. "Murky, what the *fuck*? "

I ran faster towards him, as he went full tilt into the water. It was the dead of night and the waves were crashing against the grimy Lake Michigan sand. Murky collapsed as a wave hit his body, and I dove in and grabbed him right before he disappeared completely. We both splashed powerlessly through the water. He'd fall, and I'd grab him, and just as soon as we were both upright we'd be smacked by a wave. In fleeting and astounding moments, persevering through his drunkenness, he'd reach into the water and pull me out, repeating this pattern over and over.

He coughed and wheezed a bit as I put my arms under his shoulders and finally dragged him to the shore. A few metres safe from the push and pull of the water, I laid him down and sat there, looking at the lights across the lake that shone from mysterious places I knew I'd never know the names of. I walked him back to the hotel, where mumbling, confused, and soaking wet, he passed out.

The next day, we left the motel mid-afternoon and headed east towards Sarnia. The other guys were sleeping in the back and it was only Murky and I awake, with the road ahead and the music playing. I was riding shotgun.

"Did you save me from drowning last night?" he asked under his breath. Right then it seemed really quiet. Eoin and Walter slept in the back seat, pillows against the windows, the music turned down to a faint hum to not wake them up.

I was only fumbling with the words, unsure how to respond. I'd never felt so close to death before. "I don't know, man. I'm not really sure what that was. You were wasted. I'm just glad I was there."

Murky laughed. "Crazy, hey?" he said, and glanced at me quick before looking back at the road. I gazed out the window at the passing painted lines of the highway. I couldn't believe that someone who'd come so close to death could laugh so casually about it, and I kept replaying the night's events in my mind. Despite how drunk we both had been, we'd still had the where-withal to reach into the water and pull each other out.

I laughed, too, exasperated. "Yeah," I said. "Totally fucking crazy."

Pine trees and yellow lines whizzed by as we crept closer and closer to the Canadian border. In the back seat, Walter awoke from a deep sleep, nursing off his hangover. He rubbed his eyes and yawned, stretching, intentionally hitting Eoin in the face. With a "Fuck you!" Eoin kicked him in the side, and they both laughed as Walter keeled over.

"Hey, Murk," Walter yelled out, "let's play suicide!" All three of them broke out into hysterical laughter, their eyes glassy and glazed over from exhaustion and alcohol.

"Now?" Murky said, looking at him in the rear-view mirror, shoulder-checking, side-mirror-checking, then changing lanes. "Do you want to drive?"

"Yeah, just had a good sleep, feel way better."

"Okay, one second, let me just pass this guy."

Murk sped ahead, leaving two cars in his dust, and veered back into the right-hand lane, undid his seatbelt, and put the van on cruise control.

"Okay, ready?" Murk asked Walter, on the edge of his seat in the back, ready to pounce.

"Yeah, let's do it!"

Murky lurched the chair back, so that it was reclined paral-lel to the floor, and let go of the steering wheel with one hand. Walter had gotten out of the way as the seat-back collapsed to his spot and, leaning forward, he grabbed the other side of the steering wheel. Murky crouched on the seat and Walter inched forward in a crouch, ready to take control of the brake and gas.

Murky whooped and hollered, "Okay, I'm letting go!" and, in tandem, Walter leapt forward, climbed over the collapsed chair, laughing the whole time, and assumed Murky's position in the driver's seat as Murky snaked out of the way, crawling along the horizontal chair to the back seat. The van was weaving slightly the whole time, in tiny jolts. My hands were gripped around my knees. There was a knot in the pit of my stomach as I pictured the van spinning off the road, wildly out of control.

"Smoothest one yet! What was that, under five seconds?" Murk howled from the back.

Walter raised the chair and did up his seatbelt. Murky got into his spot and put his arm around Eoin. "Must've been," Eoin smacked him on the thigh, approvingly, still laughing. "Another bullet dodged."

In a few hours, we got to the Canadian border.

"So," the border guard said, coffee in hand, as we pulled up to the window. "You've been driving to Toronto from—where? Oh, right—*Edmonton* to record an album?"

"Yeah," Walter explained, hands shaking a bit from both nerves and his hangover from the night before. "We have the contract here, I'll show you."

He reached over the dashboard and grabbed the forged recording contract that they'd written up before we'd left.

"See?" He said, just yammering on, trying to keep his cool and retain composure. "'Bloor Street Studios.' They're offering this really great deal, since they just opened up. Thousand bucks for a whole week, regardless of how long the days last. Don't you know how 'in the tank' the record industry is right now?

Officer, people really gotta go out on an arm and a leg nowadays to make a buck."

He looked at us suspiciously and took another sip from his coffee before reaching out his hand to give us back our passports. He eyed the gear in the back, the two filthy men seated amidst it, and the boxes of merch that sat atop the amplifiers and drum kit. His forefinger tapped pensively on the counter. We could tell he was thinking twice about letting us off, but I think he just was coming to the end of his shift and wanted us out of his sight as soon as possible.

"Enjoy your stay," he said, before sliding the window shut. Back on Canadian soil, we slammed our fists against the roof of the van like it was a drum, howling and laughing hysterically as Toronto waited just over the horizon.

NAUTICAL DISASTER

After a long night getting drunk, I awoke in my dorm
and wandered down to a beach called Vale Figueiras.
It was approaching noon, and the waves at this point
in the day were very high. They peaked over two or
three metres if you got out far enough, and without a
surfboard I jumped into the water to swim.

Around me was a coliseum of exposed crimson
stone that towered over the water, and all the people
running in and out of the ocean were contained by it,
at that one little point where the ocean turns to sand.
It all beamed red as the sun shattered down upon me,
as I floated in the water, and through the faint mist of
the Atlantic in the distance you could see even more
rocks, which arched like a set of fingers and a thumb.

All the surfers seemed one hundred feet out in the
water, so small I could barely make them out—though

I could tell Markus by his blond shoulder-length Austrian hair, as he would rise to a crest for a moment before crashing down then re-emerging—just bobbing, waiting for a wave, ducking in and out of that thick green salty foam, sometimes getting swallowed by that gigantic blanket of violent liquid.

I didn't know there was a limit to how far out you could go. A bit hungover and far from level-headed, I chased the waves, diving headfirst in and out and through them. My feet resting on the watery sand below, sinking to my ankles, the comforting, soft pillow of the ocean bed beneath me raising me up.

Then as the sand disappeared from under my feet, I was caught. A great weight pushed against my side and pulled me out beyond the break and I was helpless, thrashing about in the water, my joints weak and my muscles sore from the booze. I felt paralyzed as the water rose higher and higher above me.

I got smashed with a wave over a metre high and it sent me spiralling head over feet. Re-emerging, I tried to gasp for air but another wave sent me below again, and in that black, helpless moment when my eyes were closed and thoughts were clear, I accepted the fact I was going to die. With this admission, everything in me relaxed completely.

The water kept dragging me back and forth, caught in the might of its gigantic, muscular arm, whipping me out to what felt like the middle of the ocean. As my feet would briefly touch sand again, I felt jolts of relief, replaced by the feeling of some great force snatching me back out. Something invincible kept coming over me, trapped in the rise and fall, like a puppet on a string, dangling in a gale force wind. I kept being swallowed up by it till I was finally on my knees, on the shore, gasping for air, saltwater pouring from my nose and eyes, in the shallow tide with a mouth full of foam, gasping, trying to make sense of it all, disoriented, helpless.

"There is no lifeguard here," a man in a wetsuit yelled out at me.

I looked up, my eyes squinting in the sun. "Yeah, I noticed that," I answered.

"I put my wetsuit on when I saw you struggling," he said, approaching me. "You really can't go out like that beyond the break ... Where the waves start to barrel and turn white, that is already much, much too dangerous."

I nodded, kept panting, and he helped me up with an outstretched arm. I must have looked like such an idiot out there, taunting the ocean, clawing at the water like a cat trying to catch an invisible mouse. The windmills that stood atop the cliffs that overlooked Vale Figueiras pounded against the Portugal sky as the surfer helped my exhausted body back to my towel on the beach.

I thanked him and he turned his back and ran towards the waves, board in hand, disappearing from view. As I looked around on the beach, I saw I was completely alone, save for the hand of the earth cupping itself around me in the form of those faded red, towering cliffs, as the rhythm and hum of the ocean echoed against the wet, timeless sand.

KANSAS CITY BLUES

On the first tour that Eoin, Murky, Walter, and I did together, we were pulling into Kansas City after a twenty-four-hour, nonstop drive from Los Angeles. The venue was in a strip mall next to some abandoned churches and an empty parking lot. We finally opened the doors after the strange and dusty fields of the Midwest had swept across our sunken, sunset-laden eyes for an entire day and night. At one point, the moon itself was overshadowed by long crimson plateaus that stretched across Utah as far as the eye could see in every corner.

Kansas City is a desolate Southern Gothic tragedy: shuttered churches stood in grass that hadn't been mowed for what seemed like decades, and there was nobody on the streets. The shadows were eerily long, as though at the mercy of a permanent sunset, though it was still midafternoon. We showed up early for load-in. Amps were carried, assignments designated: "You set up the merch, you go meet the sound guy, you set up your drums, you order us a round." By the time six o'clock rolled around, we emerged from the darkness of sound check to the front parking lot. We were starving and we wanted barbecue.

Some local told us "Arthur Bryant's," and with that Murky drove off and returned with two full slabs of pork ribs and a pound of burnt ends. He unveiled the burgundy butcher's paper, foot still on the brake and the engine idling as he opened the driver's side door.

"Get this!" He said, black circles around his eyes, white bread in his right hand, and rib meat in his left, dipping it in sauce that was balanced on his lap under the steering wheel. He turned off the engine and spun ninety degrees in his chair, sitting up out of the vehicle in the hot Missouri air.

"You know the craziest part?" He said to us, his sixteen-hour-road-lit eyes like narrow chutes, as he tried to recall the conversation he'd just had. "I asked the clerks about Kansas City barbecue, right?" He continued, pausing only to bite and chew. "And they started going off about the rules of thumb. Essentially, the best barbecues in the United States—the only ones worth eating at—are the ones that have at one point or another burnt down."

He sat there talking, licking his fingers, and swallowing chunks of meat. Sauce was starting to form a ring around his mouth, mirroring the circles around his eyes. It was like I was staring into the face of an animal.

"The burning down, see, is an inevitability." He pointed at me with a bone held with his finger and thumb, driving home his research, his newfound insight into American barbecue culture.

"It's not the *if*, it's the *when*. If they've been around long enough, they all at some point or another go up in a big ball of lard-induced fire. It all just erupts one day, but only if there's enough grease from over the years."

"They said that, hey?" I asked, fixated on the dripping slab of ribs in between the driver and shotgun seats. I looked at the greasy keys still dangling from the ignition.

"Fuckin' right. And the craziest thing is," he chewed some more, "it's more about the idea of inevitability than it is about the idea of fire. The fire is just a symbol of the age of the place, like if it's old enough to finally have gone up in smoke, then it's old enough to uphold some traditions that newer places might not even know about, know what I mean?"

He got out a cigarette and lit it with the same greasy fingers, still covered in sauce, and small fingerprints of red juice formed around the filter, soon to be scorched slaughterhouse grease.

"Barbecue is only one hundred, one hundred fifty years old." He lit the smoke and huffed, a red ring of sauce still around his mouth. Some napkins on his lap caught a gust of wind and twirled off like dead leaves across the parking lot. "So, the barbecues that have been around long enough to finally explode and be rebuilt are the ones that really stay true to the oldest ways. Those will be the most authentic. Those will be the truest barbecues."

I asked him how many times Arthur Bryant's had burned down, if ever, but before he could answer, someone gave me a few pieces of burnt ends on white bread and my attention was driven elsewhere until showtime.

Attendance was sparse that night, one of those heartbreaking evenings where you drive an unearthly number of miles to play to nobody and not sell a single record. We hadn't even been offered a place to stay. Eoin and Walter were nowhere to be found after the show, though they were probably in the van, sharing a huge bottle of bottom-shelf in a last-ditch attempt to drink themselves to sleep while sitting upright.

Murky packed up the merch, and I coiled my cables onstage and packed my guitar as the last call bell rang. The bartender turned off the bar's stereo. What remained was an awkward silence, save for the sound of clinking glasses and the faint hiss of the kitchen's dishwasher. Murky closed a box and carried it to the van, exhausted and defeated. As he walked through the door, he glanced over at me with a faint smile. I wondered then if there was any kind of limit to how many times a barbecue place could be burned down before they stopped building it back up.

DOGS

In Portugal there are dogs everywhere. Wild, stray dogs, running alongside city traffic, even coming into the bars—and treated like patrons in some cases. They're neighbourhood characters, born into the bondage of homelessness, fighting their entire lives for scraps.

They roam bars and restaurants during service, looking for handouts and mugging for food, pets, and smiles, and then they follow the smokers out onto the street to curl up at the feet of strangers. They're kind and affectionate the way all house dogs are, except patches of dirt and shit cover the spots of hair missing from their mangy fur. Maybe these dogs are the reincarnated souls of dead surfers, I thought, forever indebted to the ocean, that unimaginable might that even in these new lives they couldn't turn their backs to.

"Right now, we're about three hundred kilometres from Africa as the crow flies," said Koen, a Dutchman who'd come to the camp for the summer, who sat me down by the water later that night and rolled me a smoke. "You're far away from the rest of Europe. Think about it."

Earlier that evening, before sunset, Markus and I were on the beach and getting ready to head back to camp. He started yelling at another surfer, pointing out to the waves. They hollered back and forth in German at each other, and when I squinted into the sun, I could see something very dark and far away bobbing up and down in the water, rising and falling, like what could've been a person, long since drowned.

The surfer lowered his binoculars and said something to Markus before grabbing his board and running off into the water, frantically paddling out to rescue whatever it was that was floating out there. When he came back to shore ten minutes later, he was holding this strange foam floater that had an algae-covered rope dangling from the end of it that must've been about fifty feet long. We stood there, three of us in the sand, pulling on the rope to try to find the end. The floater was perfectly cut and shaped for buoyancy and riding the waves as elegantly as a seasick traveller, a twisted shrine of garbage, thrashing about in the ocean. Koen explained to me what it was.

"Isn't it obvious?" He laughed into his wine. "There was a brick of hash on the end of that thing at some point. Some Moroccan tied his drugs to the end and threw it off the side of a boat towards Europe."

He explained to me the knowledge these guys have of the ocean. How when they drop the package from a tiny motorboat miles away from shore in the cover of darkness, under the hood of that big, black night, it always ends up in the right hands.

"The receiver probably found the package at sea, pulled the line, cut the brick of hash off the end, and threw the floater back in the water," Koen said. "Hash used to be so common here, all Europe's hash landed in Portugal. Now Interpol is patrolling the waters so all you can get is weed that's grown here. That thing that washed up today, that's probably months, if not years, old."

Koen got up for a second and got us each a beer.

"What else would it be?" he said upon return. "Today, you found the corpse of a successful drug smuggling mission. And thank god, because we need to get our hash somehow . . ."

We talked some more, then I thanked him for the beer and made my way once more up the hill to the bar. A barking dog ran across the street, pissed on a wall, glanced up at me, and ran off into the night, back down that spiralling path towards the beach. Inside, I found Johnny, an Australian instructor, and sat next to him.

"I've been teaching beginner surfers for about six years," he said to me, right up to my ear, over the pounding hum of the music playing over the bar speakers. "Not a day goes by when I'm not in the water. By the end of the week, your whole body just aches. The saltwater, the paddling, staying up on your board; your skin, your muscles . . . it kills you."

The conversation moved to talk of waves. I had learned quickly that surfers love bragging about the waves they've seen and rode. Where in the world the biggest are, what time of year to hit the water, who they've rode the waves with, and so on.

"I'll let you in on two secrets about surfers," he said, pulling on his beer. "First of all, the craziest sessions always happen on Wednesdays. It's kind of a surfer's legend. No one can explain it. Wednesdays always have the highest waves. Rule of thumb, always surf Wednesday tides."

He started rolling a cigarette. I thought of how no musician on tour can justify not playing from Thursday to Sunday, how the week begins at a lull on Monday and Tuesday and gradually crescendoes into the beating heart of the weekend. Fridays and Saturdays have the best shows, Sundays are the natural comedown, and the repetitive, monotonous cycle continues the following morning.

"Another thing." His Australian accent was really coming out now, and he lit his smoke. "Surfers have terrible reputations. Sexually, I mean. Everyone says we're these slutty idiots. STDs, pregnancies, all that shit, you name it. People say we're *pigs*, y'know? People say we never wrap it up, that you'll always get the clap from a surfer. But, the truth?"

He smirked and leaned in closer, putting his hand on my shoulder.

"The truth is that rubbers always break because there's always bits of sand on your cock." He gave me a slight jab in the ribs with his elbow, winked at me, finished his beer with a burp, and with a curt, "I gotta piss," Johnny disappeared into the crowd. In the cool night air, the faint sound of barking dogs drifted upwards from the beach.

DON'T MAKE LIFE DECISIONS WHEN YOU'RE DRUNK AND INSANE

That's probably the best advice you can give someone about going on tour. Don't sell or buy a house. Don't drop out of school. Don't break up with your girlfriend. Don't tell your friends you hate them. Don't break up the band. If you're going to do those things, wait until you fucking get home. Stay put, hold steady, and, above all, finish the tour. You'll be there soon.

You've been breathing the same stale air as three other people for two weeks. You've lived less than three feet away from all of them and, like it or not, you depend on each other for survival. You borrow and steal from them and they borrow and steal from you. You share drinks and smokes. You live in an intimacy that knows no bounds within the rigid confines of the van doors. You share memories and mixed emotions. Your eyes are a thick crimson. Your faces unrecognizable. You share secrets and there are no secrets between you. You smell like each other. You start to talk and look the same. Your hearts and minds beat as one and there is no escape. Despite how their jokes, dirty clothes, and drinking habits disgust you, your life depends on them. There is no going home.

At many times on many tours, I have repeated this mantra: "Don't make life decisions when you're drunk and insane. Don't make life decisions when you're drunk and insane. Don't make life decisions . . ."

I've had to recite it to myself in my own mind, the music playing from the car stereo speakers in the front. Over and over again, over the seemingly infinite curving highway that connects Winnipeg to Toronto on the Canadian Shield, or heading northeast towards the heartland of the USA from a day spent battling Los Angeles rush hour traffic, playing show after show after show.

"Yeah, sure, you can have one of my beers—but make sure you buy the next case."

"You really asking for a hit off this joint? I'm down to my last pinch."

"I mean, you can have a smoke—but try to remember that I've only got two left."

"You guys, come on, you've got to be more careful. You almost spilled beer on my pedal board."

"Don't put drinks on my amp! How many fuckin' times do I have to tell you?"

And it goes on like that, in tiny, tiny increments. All day long. Until you play. And then, there's that window where the illusions of the show descend onto the stage like a curtain and wraps in it even the performers who are putting it on. The illusion of the stage lights, of the voluminous amplifiers, of the sweat and energy: everyone, let alone the audience, forgets about the drive to the show and the long, sweaty haul up the stairs with a drum kit, instruments, and speaker cabinets in hand.

This is the illusion that the ticket holder is paying for. You pay the cover to experience a magic show, where all connection to reality is lost. You pay to believe that the band has transmogrified into existence before you. You pay to see transcendence. You pay to believe that the very stage on which they stand would not even exist without the musicians it supports.

The audience doesn't even know that the load-in happened. To them, the practicality of touring is an irrelevant, nonexistent thing. The band magically appears in front of the eager crowd, emerging from the haze, for which there is no fog machine. The band basks under the heat of lights, which have no fixtures; plays effortlessly, perfectly; and then descends into the darkness of a backstage world that must be another dimension, occupying another form of time and space. The crowd members pay their tab, clasp their ticket stubs tightly between their fingers, and leave the room.

The instruments, all night, have changed their own strings. The tour bus has done its own driving. The band is transported directly to tomorrow through the portal that is the greenroom door. The amps unplug themselves, put themselves in their road cases, and give themselves a pat on the back when they've lugged themselves up and down those taunting, steep stairs. The money appears in the bank account magically at the end of the tour, no one has even met or exchanged names—the promoter, if he exists at all, is an entity that merely oversees the unfolding of this secret magic, unbeknownst to the nameless faces in the audience.

The merch sets itself up, the t-shirts hang themselves on hangers, and the records lay themselves out on the table. They decide their own price, and they write it on the back of a cracked beer coaster with a fine-tipped Sharpie every night before every show. The lyrics even write themselves, and the music hangs disembodied, emanating from the speakers that didn't even exist before the doors opened.

In such a world, there exists no in-between. There is no long drive, no carrying of the gear, no haul. There is no exhaustion, no hangover, no sleepless night. There is no stench in the van. There are no dirty fingernails. No body odour, no greasy hair, no anger or fist fights or sexual jealousy. No depression or disappointment.

A good band can do this, and an even better band does it to itself. But after that one half-hour span of bodiless energy every night, you return to reality. You have to load out. You have to remember where you parked the van. You have to finish your beer and sober up enough to carry your amps. You have to settle with the promoter, and you have to remember his name. You have to get your shit together. And you have to let all the subtle annoyances of your bandmates slide right off your back.

"Where did you put my cables? I don't mind that you use them, but—"

"Is all the beer from backstage gone? Who drank the last one?"

"I can't smoke a dart in the van . . . ? You guys have been smoking weed in here all fucking day."

"Yeah, I'll move my shit, just gimme a second . . ."

It's always the middle of the tour when the tensions are highest, but the band is playing its best. When that curtain of illusion and deception is heaviest, where you forget for that half-hour that you're even a musician, that there's something physical and muscular that's making you play those notes. Mark it on a calendar; those three shows that lie right in the middle of a long stretch of dates are the pinnacle. Not the first shows, by any means, and definitely not the last ones: it's the middle. Your rhythm is inarguable. You're completely connected to the music, and also, unfortunately at times, to each other. This is when you feel the most, and least, alone.

At night, you lay awake, sometimes for hours on end. Surrounded by snoring bodies, chests rising and falling in drunken anesthesia. There are no dreams being had by anybody here. "Every time I sleep on a floor," you keep telling yourself, "every time a promoter shorts us, every time we get ripped off by a headlining band, every time we play a show to nobody except the bartender and his girlfriend: that's one step closer to that time being our last. Don't make life decisions when you're drunk and insane. Don't make life decisions when you're drunk and insane. Don't make life decisions . . ."

You say it over and over to yourself, almost hypnotically, and it's the comforting rhythm of that mantra that finally, gracefully, puts you to sleep.

ARRIVAL

I woke up the next morning to the hot Portuguese sun announcing that this was the day that the band was arriving. After their plane had landed at Heathrow they'd taken the Tube straight into the city, met the van rental company, driven through rush hour traffic on the Westway to grab their backline and merch from the label's office in the rainy mid-September smog, navigated London traffic to the A20 towards Dover, and got on the last ferry to Calais by eleven p.m., where they killed a few more hours on the Route nationale.

After a short night's sleep somewhere in France, they hit the van and drove to Paris for a quick pit stop so Davey could meet a friend to grab a package of hash that he planned on lasting him through the tour, so that was the second day in a row of bumper-to-bumper traffic, stranded in the gridlock of the French capital, with time on the clock ticking idly by.

By early evening, they finally left Paris behind and headed south where they killed six or seven more hours to end up in the south of France for a night in a roadside alpine motel. By the time they'd crossed the Spain-Portugal border, they'd been in transit for three straight days. Four countries, countless dialects, and a whole lot of wasted time.

Markus organized the night's show as a send-off for the surfers at the end of the season. It'd be the next day before we'd be in Lisbon, but something deep inside me felt like I'd already left the ocean. A new long-haul for me was now beginning, with only two days' rest in between this one and the last.

They showed up around three in the afternoon and looked as haggard as beasts. The massive blue Sprinter van knocked up dust as it approached, towering over the dirty back road, standing as tall as a wave in water. I ran out to them, excited, still in disbelief that we were finally all on this continent together.

"Get us out of the fucking van," I heard someone yell, and with a bang of the driver's side door, there he was: Davey Moodey, more or less collapsing to the ground. His sunglasses stayed on his head the whole time. Davey had on a denim jacket that looked straight off the hanger of the clothing store that he'd bought it from, brand new, in the hot, Portuguese sun. Harrison Pool, bass and backing vocals, emerged from his back seat a sweaty, unshaven mess, holding two beers champion-high as a cigarette dangled from his mouth. Our drummer, Gerry Mortarino—who slept during pretty much every drive and barely ever spoke—rubbed sleep from his eyes as he climbed out of the back. London to Portugal in half a week: highway tolls, sleepless nights, expensive gas, hotel rooms, temperatures and elevations rising and falling while the white lines of the highway pound against the corners of your eyes as the road goes on and on.

"Three fucking days dude!" Davey said, *"Three fucking days!"*

Markus greeted them all and couldn't believe it.

"You guys *must* be Canadian," he said, laughing. "I cannot believe you drove from London. Fucking *London!*"

"Hop, skip, and a jump for us, man," Davey replied, hash joint already sparked. We were laughing hysterically. The sun was going to start setting soon, and we had to load our gear. Davey pulled the van around to the bandshell where we'd be playing and we started hauling everything under the tent. By now, it was around six thirty and the sun was barely hanging off the side of the horizon line, ready to descend into the confines of night.

We were done sound check by half seven. It was going to be loud. By now, surfers from all over Costa Vicentina had congregated, the sound of guitars through the landscape like a beckoning call, and everyone was getting drunk. A haze of weed and hash smoke ascended into the sky as stars appeared like cap gun shells, popping off one by one. I took a drag off someone's spliff and poured myself a glass of wine.

Gerry was lying down in the van, Davey was talking to girls by the bar, and Harrison was making his way through the sand towards me, materializing in the dark evening like a ghost. "Fuck, man," he said, "I gotta talk to you." He guided me towards the stage and put his drink down on his amplifier. His eyes were like pinpricks, piercing mine. "Holy fuck, man," he said, crossing his arms. "That was hell. That drive was fucking hell."

I laughed. "I can only imagine!" I patted him on the back, as though we were in an English pub; I thought, a part of his mind must still be back in the UK anyway, might as well make the transition a bit more gradual. I tried to clear the tension in the moment with some placid laughter. "I still don't know how I got out of that one."

"Well, no shit," Harrison said, re-intensifying the conversation. "You think I didn't want to be hanging out on a fucking beach with you the past few days? I kept asking myself, as we got roped into that bullshit misadventure of Davey's: why the fuck am I here?"

"What do you mean? Why didn't you just fly into Lisbon in the first place and come meet me?" I asked, my brow furrowed.

"Don't you know Davey, man?" he said, rhetorically. "He's never given you that speech? 'My fuckin' band, my fuckin' way,' all that bullshit. If he could've convinced you to not play those last few shows back home, you would've been in on the ride too."

Harrison paused for a second, gathering his words, and then the verbal floodgates opened. "Truth is, I told him I didn't want to go to Paris. He booked our flights and made us go with him, to pick up that fucking package, meet his sketchy dealer in Sarcelles. You think I wanted to have anything to do with that? It added a whole fucking day of driving onto our trip. By the time we were one hundred clicks from here, I was ready to fucking burst. I was *trapped* in that fucking van, man; I was so fucking mad. Totally trapped. You were on tour, so you had a way out, lucky prick."

"Why didn't you just say that to him?" I asked, slamming my wine. "I would've."

"I did, man," he said. "We kind of got into it. It almost came to blows. You know what he told me, in Paris? He said: 'You don't like it, get the fuck out of the van.' He gave me that whole speech, that whole 'my way or the highway' speech. And I had no choice but to get back in after butting heads. This is the only band I tour with. It was really shitty. I was totally *trapped*."

Harrison paused again, eyes wide, staring into mine.

"When it comes down to it, he just didn't want to be alone for pickups in London, I guess. Misery loves company, or however the saying goes. Or maybe Davey just loves the control."

I kept letting him talk, letting him get out whatever he needed to. "I also learned something kind of weird about him, at the UK border." He lit a smoke and took a drag. "I saw our work permits: all of our birth dates, laid out there one-by-one. And Davey?" He looked away, off into the night. "Davey's got a good *twenty years* on all of us. I had no idea, man. What the fuck? He's easily *twenty years* our senior? I mean, five years, fuck; *ten*, even. But *twenty*? And why has he never told me that before? What the fuck is this guy doing, recruiting a bunch of kids to do his tours for him? It's like he's surviving on the backs of these younger people, desperate for an avenue to stay relevant—"

I lowered my glass to his amp with a clink and put my hand back on his shoulder, trying to calm the guy down. "Well," I said, interrupting. "You're here now. You're just pissed off from the drive. Try not to let it get to you. We've got a hell of a road ahead of us. And this is a good opportunity."

"For sure," he said, sighing: the relief was apparent in his shoulders, how they dropped, loosened up a bit, now that he'd gotten this off his chest. "Just don't let him walk all over you, if you can help it. Also, I'm in a fuckin' bad mood. I lost my favourite Black Flag shirt. Last I saw, it was on the floor of the van, and then it just disa—"

From the shadows, a voice broke in. "I can't believe you have to leave tomorrow," Markus said, appearing out of nowhere and giving me a hug.

"You're telling me," I said, wrapping my arms around him too. "It seems like I just got here. I can't believe this tour is actually starting. The last two days have felt like I've been lost in a dream."

It was going to be a long run. After Lisbon, the city everybody raved about in its legendary capacity for booze and drugs, we were to go inland to the wild circuses of Madrid and Barcelona, then up through the French Alps before heading northwest after Paris towards the Chunnel in Calais. A long stretch of dates in the UK and Ireland preceded our worming our way back to the continent for weeks of shows in Germany, Austria, the Czech Republic, Hungary, and Belgium, before flying out of London right at the verge of winter. Davey planned on staying an extra week, fresh off another long successful tour with a young band in tow, to shop around a new record and follow up on some meetings scheduled with labels, agents, and managers in London. *This could be the start of something huge,* I remember thinking. *The tour I've been waiting for. But right now, before it's even begun, it feels like it has no end.*

I looked over my shoulder at the van, headlights off, sitting there motionless, next to the tent and thought about how that would be my home for the next stretch of weeks. Only in music are you pushed and pulled from where you are, as tight grips form around you and throw you where the songs want to take you. Under a starlit sky, as the ocean waves crashed against the edge of Europe, I walked up to the van windows and looked inside. *If not for the songs,* I thought, *I'd never have arrived here, but also, I'd probably never leave.* Around Gerry, the band's bags were strewn across the seats, and mine would be there, too, as of tomorrow morning.

SARNIA

On the last tour that Eoin, Murky, Walter, and I were on together, we were in Michigan again, barrelling towards Sarnia, for the start of another week of dates in Southern Ontario. We were running late: a half-hour from the border, and we played in less than three, so like every night for as long as we could remember, we passed around a bottle, taking swigs to get ready for the set. We had a sixty of bottom-shelf that was leaning towards completion and an un-cracked two-six of Yukon Jack that Walter had stolen from the liquor outlet in Michigan that we'd bought the sixty-pounder from.

The towers of the Sarnia chemical plants stood tall like artifacts of an ancient civilization. We could see them in the distance from across the St.

Clair River, blinking in a cancerous Morse code. The first thing I noticed was the smokestacks, then the winding, effervescent pipes of the chemical facilities basking in a neon glow that grew stronger as we inched closer and closer to Canada, the air thickening as Sarnia's strange, aluminum smell got more pungent and toxic with our approach. All those cubic, tangled messes of massive, sprawling poisonous factories, that was what signalled our arrival home. Sarnia grew closer in slow motion, a grainy, dystopic vision of Southern Ontario, seen through the smudgy and oily lens of the windshield, splattered with dead bugs and splintered with cracks from stray highway pebbles.

We were drunk enough to start smoking inside the van. Eoin had a pack of American cigarettes that he'd swiped from a house party a few nights earlier, and although none of us considered ourselves smokers at the time, there was always this threshold in our inebriation where we'd say "fuck it" and light some up. We were all laughing our asses off, singing along with the radio at the top of our lungs, little trails of smoke and red embers exiting the van as we ashed through the cracks in the windows. The sun was setting behind us, the rear- and side-view mirrors illuminated with a sliver of yellowy orange at the bottom of the sky.

At one point, Eoin reached down to his feet. "Hey, man, is this yours?" He held up a filthy Black Flag shirt. "Love this fucking band, man! Didn't see that you had this."

I shook my head. "No, not mine," I said, reaching out for it, spreading open the arms. "Great shirt, though. Where'd you find it?"

"Just noticed it now, showed up on the floor of the van here. Someone from the opening band must've changed shirts when they were partying in here the other night."

"You like all their later stuff too? When they got all weird? Like, *Process of Weeding Out*? Or are you a *First Four Years* kind of fan?"

"I love it all." Eoin took a swig from the bottle. "Here, give that back over, I want to see if it fits—"

"Hey, turn that up!" Walter reached from the back seat to the radio, turning the volume knob on a distorted stew of static and music. We had started picking up a Canadian radio station, so he adjusted the dial, moving it back and forth until the sound was crystal clear. "You remember this band? I used to love this song!"

"Yeah, what the fuck were they called?" Eoin asked, taking another swig. "Some fucking Vancouver band, from the nineties. Fuck, this is going to drive me crazy." Murk and Eoin got in a long argument, which from my place in the back seat got swallowed up by the music. I was too young to know who wrote the song, a mid-level chart hit on Canadian FM radio from 1996, and I barely recognized it—and then with the screech of the tires, there was an enormous crash and the body of a deer slammed against our windshield. All of us screamed as we saw one yellow, terrified eye gaze into ours for just a split second, in shock from the blinding headlights and howling brakes that had paralyzed it in the middle of the highway. Murky turned the steering wheel sharp to the left, and the van fishtailed hard on the road, spinning at full speed.

I couldn't breathe. It was like being caught in an oceanic wave, spinning around like a washing machine; a circular, uncontrollable motion. There was a strange sense of calm that came over me as I accepted that this was how I was going to die.

Somehow Murky regained control, and the van ground to a halt. We were completely stopped in the middle of a two-lane highway, and we started yelling at him to head to the shoulder.

The front of the van was a mangled mess. Eoin shouted again from the shotgun seat to pull over, Murky hollered back at him, spinning the wheel to the right and veering the van to the side of the road.

All of us were in shock. As Murky took the keys from the ignition, we piled out of the van. The body of the deer was a red smear on the asphalt about two hundred yards away, deadly still and barely even able to make it out from the flashing hazard lights.

That's when the floodgates really opened. "What the *fuck*, Murk?" Eoin yelled at him. "What the fuck were you doing?"

"What do you mean?" Murky shouted back. "What are you talking about?"

"You didn't see that fucking deer? You couldn't have stopped any sooner?" Their voices were echoing through the Michigan woods now. "What the fuck is wrong with you, man?"

"What the *fuck* is wrong with *me*?" Murky spat, "You don't even fucking *drive*! You guys were all drinking and screaming in that fucking van, I could barely concentrate on the road—now look at that fucking thing!" Murky gestured towards the wreck, its smoky hood and raw wheels heating up the air around it.

"For fuck's sake, don't you even fucking start," Eoin said, walking towards the back seat. He opened the back door, reached in, and grabbed the bottle of Yukon Jack that was lying on the floor. "You're a fucking baby. You were drinking, too, you fuckin' hypocrite."

Murky was really fuming now, I could see it in his eyes. Walter and I stood back, watching this unfold, and we heard the crack of the lid of the bottle. Eoin took a huge swig, easily two or three shots in one, and closed the cap. "You're a fucking pussy. A fucking *faggot*. Shut your mouth, do your job, and learn how to fucking drive."

Murky's fist connected with Eoin square in the jaw—we heard the impact—and Eoin's feet seemed to leave the ground entirely, and he landed on his back, cradling the Yukon Jack the whole time. Walter and I ran over to the two of them. I was pulled Murky away, screaming for them to stop, while Walter helped Eoin to his feet.

"Guys, guys, *guys!*" I yelled, as Eoin laughed condescendingly. He lunged forward but Walter held him back. "Stop it, *both* of you!"

A few minutes passed, and we took them to either side of the demolished van, each of them cursing at the other like it was some kind of soundproof buffer. Walter and I tried to calm them both down, as headlights in the distance poked over the road. The sound of four tires slowing down on concrete had never been so comforting.

The driver ground to a halt next to us and rolled his window down. "Looks like you boys need some help."

After what seemed like hours, the cops that were called finally showed up to the scene. We dragged the dead deer to the side of the road and thanked the driver, who drove off, disappearing into the night. The cops called us a tow truck, and Eoin, who'd been hiding the bottle of Yukon Jack the entire time and sneaking pulls, threw the empty into the ditch where it vanished from view. Murky and I rode up front with the tow truck driver, and Walter and Eoin rode in the squad car.

Defeated, we climbed out of the vehicles at the border and the cops said goodbye. Empty McDonald's boxes and cups rolled out with Eoin and Walter as they exited the car. Like we'd done so many times before, we showed the border guard our wrinkled forged recording contract. The tow truck driver released the metal hook, and the van crashed to the ground, and without even a goodbye he was back across the border and off.

"Well," Walter shrugged, gesturing at the wreck. "What are we gonna do?"

Everyone was silent. I went to sit down on a curb and put my face in my hands. It was past eleven o'clock by now. We'd missed our show in Sarnia by hours, but we still had a radio appearance on a college station in Toronto the next morning.

"Well, we have to get to the city," I said, rubbing my eyes. "We have to make that radio show. Plus, we have a place to stay there. Can we buy a new van in Toronto? Or rent one or something? I can call my folks and see if they can wire me some money—"

Eoin cut me off. "Here's what we're doing," he said, grabbing his bag and guitar, and checking to make sure everything was there. "I'm hitchhiking to the city. You guys stay behind and find a new vehicle, figure this shit out. Our show isn't till tomorrow night, and even the morning radio interview isn't till ten, so that gives me almost twelve hours to get there."

Eoin opened the back door of the van for a quick dummy check, and then turned around and faced us again. "If you want to come, you can," he said, pointing right at me.

"*What?*" Murky said, then looked to Walter.

"What the fuck are you talking about?" Walter said, shocked. "What about us?"

Eoin laughed. "Give me a fucking break," he said, lifting his guitar and bag up to his shoulders. "We can do the session alone. Two guitars. Obviously, this is the answer."

"So what, we're supposed to just fucking stay here in Sarnia? Where the fuck are we going to go? What the *fuck* are we going to do?"

"I don't know. This is on you now, man. Let me know when you figure it out," he said, walking away from the border, but not turning his back on Walter and Murky until he pointed at me first, beckoning me to follow. "You: let's fucking *go.*"

I looked silently at both of them. I held out my arms, not sure what to say.

Murky was pacing, fuming. I couldn't even look him in the eyes as I left. After a few minutes, I got the courage to turn around for a glance, but he and Walter weren't at the van; they'd probably wandered off to find a bar, use a phone, gather their senses, and find a place to stay. The wreckage, an empty, dead piece of metal, just stayed put in its parking spot at the border, the toxic orange hue of Sarnia's chemical plant lights reflecting ominously off its twisted hood.

Sobering up with every step, Eoin and I made it to the 402 and held out our thumbs. Hours passed. It had to be at least three a.m. by the time, finally, a trucker pulled over.

"Where are you headed?" he asked us.

"Toronto," we both said, exasperated, but in unison.

"I can get you to Pearson Airport." He said, glancing back and forth between us and the road. It was the dead of summer, so the sky was already starting to turn from pitch black to navy blue. "That work?"

Without even answering, we climbed in.

"There's a four-litre of water in the back," the trucker said, turning off his hazards and pulling into the right-hand lane. "And you can both crash on my bed."

"Thank you so much," we repeated. Eoin and I both collapsed, somehow fitting together on that small, hard truck mattress like oily sardines in a tin can. He said quietly to me, barely audible: "You made the right choice. We have *our* careers to think about."

From the driver's seat I vaguely heard, "I'll wake you up when I get there. You both look like shit, get some sl—"

RESCUE

We woke to the gongs of hangovers ringing in our minds, all snapped upright in bed, and began heaving amplifiers and bass drums into our Sprinter van. Before hitting the autoestrada, we stopped for a round of goodbyes at the beach.

I saw Markus there, by the camp's beach headquarters: a wood shack with a tin roof and all the gear you'd need for a day on the waves, which they rented out to camp residents and walk-ups alike. People came in and out of it for hours, grabbing stuff to take out onto the water. Those who'd just rode in from a session would chill out and catch their breath before heading up the hill to the pub that overlooked the ocean. There, they could quietly replay the day's crashing and churning of

Atlantic water with a calm, still bottle of Sagres in their fingers.

Markus looked rough—just as hungover as the rest of us.

"What a night!" he said. "The band was so *loud!* So awesome!"

We all shared a round of hugs and agreed to meet up in Vienna soon. Markus and I walked away from the others and talked about my last few days, about the ocean, about surfing, about the great people who came from all corners of Europe. It was hard to leave.

"It's been so great being here," I said, "taking a break, you know? I'm just always on the road, always moving at a thousand clicks. It's been such a relief, like the calm before the storm, as they say. I just wish I could've been a natural surfer, like you guys . . . to even be able to stand on the board. You make it look so easy. It's beautiful. I gotta say, I'm jealous."

Someone called over to Markus, waving a spliff in the air, the smoke signalling us to join. He ran up to us and passed it to Markus, who took a quick hit before it made its way back to everybody else.

"When I started, you know," he finally replied, his eyes darting back to me, "for like one whole year, I couldn't even pop up."

I tried to imagine Markus struggling out there, in the middle of the ocean, and I just couldn't. He was one of those guys who seemed to be good at everything. Days before, I watched him fly above the rip like a bird of prey and glide in to shore so effortlessly: it was as though he'd been put on this earth to do it. I thought about a younger Markus, a pale, skinnier Austrian boy falling off his board time and again, and I just couldn't see it.

Markus continued, "The strength it takes, the determination, the pain and fear—all the times I've almost drowned, and still got back up. I had to work at it for what seemed like forever, even just to get the courage to lie on the board and paddle out. Years and years and years went into the moment I first stood up, and when I rode the waves all the way to shore, it was like everything I'd ever wanted. I just never gave up."

It was midday. The waves were high. I walked alone down the beach to where the tide was pushing and pulling against the sand, and I approached the ocean cautiously this time, my fearful respect inspired by a knowledge of how it might feel to drown. The band was up by the van, changing their clothes, lying in the sun, nursing their hangovers with plastic bottles of Évian and Vittel.

Then, in the distance, beyond the break, I could make out the shape of someone struggling in the waves, being thrashed about, and right away I knew the signs. She helplessly raised and lowered her arms trying to get the attention of the beachgoers, but the people, transfixed by the crispness of their cervejas and the heat of the sun glaring down on them, didn't notice a thing.

I had a flashback to tumbling about in that washing machine, with a mouthful of salt and foam, the fear that gripped my muscles and bones, unable to breathe, and I ran, screaming, towards a surfer.

"Get your board!" I yelled, pointing out to her. "She needs help!"

He looked at me, then at her, bolted into the water, and ducked under a wave to paddle out. Within a minute she was up on his board and safe, and she thanked me as he wrapped her shaking body in a towel upon hitting the shore.

I kept playing that moment in the water over again in my head. Tumbling and circling, splashing helplessly in the waves in the total darkness of eyes clamped shut. So strange to think back and realize how easily it could have gone the other way, when the ocean floor drops out from under you and there's no escape as you're pulled outwards by a gigantic furious hand. At the mercy of the elements, I knew exactly what had gone through her mind: if you struggle, it shows no pity, only wraps you in a fluid bondage and takes you as its captive.

I watched her briefly as she gathered her things and walked back up the hill towards her car. Meanwhile the band, coming down from the van, passed her, unaware, on the path. I was sitting alone in the sand, staring off into the ocean.

"You okay?" Davey asked.

"Yeah, I think so."

We stayed there only a few minutes more, giving one last long look out into the Atlantic waves, thinking about who and what it would next make its prisoner.

TORONTO

Everything that Eoin, Murky, or Walter did, they did with an unparalleled ferocity. Whether it was learning how to play a song together or drinking a bottle of rye, once they started, there really was no turning back. The switch was either on or off and they knew only one speed. For better or for worse, they were worn hard by their own intensity when it came to their outlooks on life. If anything stood in their way—whether a deer on the highway or a promoter in a club—it would be run over, and there was no turning back.

Eoin and I had made it to the radio show, and somehow Murky and Walter had found a van. Murk's mom wired him some money, and with that and the little cash we had from merch sales and tour revenue, they were back on the road by early afternoon the next day.

Murky and Walter pulled up to the venue in Toronto a few minutes before sound check in—oddly enough—another Ford Windstar, this one considerably less silver than its predecessor. We loaded in with a fury none of us had felt before. We were all so happy to be together again. Eoin and Murk barely spoke about the confrontation in Michigan; it seemed like the hatchet was buried, and we were forward-looking, impatient to play the show.

Murky, totally exhausted and not in the mood for a night out, went home with a girl not too long after we finished our set, telling us he'd meet back up with us in the morning wherever we were staying. "Might be good to catch up on some sleep, guys," Murk said, as he shut the driver's side door and drove off west down Queen. Eoin, Walter, and I, on the other hand, went out to celebrate: we bought speed at a College and Spadina afterhours, from a dealer who sold me eight hits for the price of six back home. There was a girl named Peppermint in knee-high leather boots dancing around the place and the DJ played techno at an obnoxiously loud volume.

"You want *drugs?*" the dealer asked me, as he slammed cans of Budweiser, yelling in my ear over the pounding of the 808. His pupils were the size of dinner plates. I told him I wanted ecstasy and he handed me eight small green pills. I took two immediately and went off to find the guys.

A few hours passed and we were in a basement apartment on Dupont. The sun was long coming up and we were drinking rye and ginger to try to come down and maybe get a few hours' sleep. It wasn't happening.

"Guess this wasn't MDMA," we kept saying to each other, that impure, speedy rush boiling up from inside of us. What we talked about, you couldn't be sure—in those nights and mornings, words are spoken, but nothing is said. Just nonsensical, illogical gibberish: opinions on politics, music, sex, and culture that have little to no basis in fact.

Finally, Murky arrived in the late morning and rounded us all up. "What the *fuck*, you guys!" he exclaimed. "C'mon—we gotta go."

He got behind the wheel and kept silent the whole time, as Eoin, Walter, and I, still high and drunk as fuck from the night before, put towels over our heads, trying to laugh away the black cloud of impending doom. I was hallucinating, talking to the sun and moon as I pictured them in my mind, circling above me in the sky like two black helicopters.

Eoin was in the back seat, bottle of rye in his right hand and bottle of ginger ale in his left, demanding we put on the Replacements and crank it. "It's gotta be *Let It Be*," he was saying, his eyes big and black and dark. "I can only listen to the Replacements at a time like this."

Murk was still angry, silently stewing in the driver's seat. My hands shaking, I opened up the CD case, with that photo of the four Replacements sitting on a rooftop on the front, and put the disc in the stereo. Eoin continued on, talking at racehorse speed to nobody in particular. "I don't usually say that. I save the Replacements for special occasions. But now we kind of need this."

He trailed off, and Murky pulled onto the 401. Walter, momentarily suicidal in his amphetamine comedown, opened the back door and tried to jump out of the van. "No! What the fuck are you doing?" we yelled and grabbed him, and he sat back down, sweating everywhere and laughing hysterically like it was all some big joke.

No one slept or passed out on the way to Ottawa. Murky drove right up to the door of the venue as the sun started going down, and by now Eoin, Walter, and I had been up for almost forty-eight hours. Murky and I carried every piece of equipment up two long flights of stairs, my muscles shaking and weak with booze, speed, and guilt. Eoin and Walter stayed in the van, trembling in the back. It was one of those times where you're really not sure how you're going to be able to play a single note.

But, we did it—we got through the show thanks to a masochistic work ethic and the help of copious amounts of whiskey. Onstage that night I experienced a kind of transformation, where as soon as a guitar's in your hand, somehow you're totally rejuvenated. Hungover, coming down, or sick with the flu: all your problems find a way to frantically leave your body as the music enters, as though they're getting violently thrown out of a packed nightclub by a huge bouncer. It only happens when you're young, and when it does, it feels like invincibility.

We got through both sets, and Murky, the only one not pummelled from the night before, walked around the venue, just happy to have gotten through another bizarre day on the road, but nonetheless pissed off about getting stuck once again with the entire day's drive and load-in.

"Hey, Murk," I said to him, as we packed up our things together onstage. "I'm sorry, man. We didn't know what we were buying. We thought it was ecstasy. We were just happy to be all back together after what happened in Michigan—"

"Man, I don't want to hear it. For the second day in a row, you left me completely fucking alone."

We organized the gear onstage in an awkward silence. As the venue emptied and the bartender turned the house lights on, I tried to tell him I'd go and settle but he cut me off.

"Hey, Walter," Murky yelled across the room, "you going to a bar tonight?"

Walter turned and looked back at him, his black-saucer eyes dead and lifeless. "Well, *yeah*," he said, menacingly. He seemed eager to get more drinks in him, soften the blow of what was turning out to be a never-ending comedown. "Obviously."

I went over to the bar where the promoter was counting money with the guy behind the till, hopeful we could hit the road, load out the gear, and leave this day and night from hell behind us. It was getting worse, that feeling where the drugs are leaving your body—you'd swear you can even feel them worming out of your bloodstream when you piss—and the subconscious mind has this horrifying realization that the end of its high is near.

"Hey, man, can we settle?" I asked him.

The promoter looked at me coyly.

"You know," he said, putting an elbow on the bar and picking up his gin and tonic with the other hand, "there's no money. But, if you *want*, I can make it all worth your while in some other way."

I looked at him, confused. "What are you saying, exactly?"

"Well, you know." He took a sip of his drink. I could tell that he, too, was flying pretty high—his eyes, those big, black, dinner plates that I'd seen all night in Toronto. "I can make a couple phone calls. And upstairs there's a strip club . . ."

I looked at him, furrowed my brow.

"Are you for real, man?" I said. "I'd rather just get the fucking money and go."

He shook his head and shrugged. He went back to talking to the bartender, done with me. I thanked him for nothing and found Murky.

"Let's get the fuck outta here," I said to him. "Fuck this day."

He laughed, and we pulled the last piece of gear off the stage and loaded it in the van, he put the keys in the ignition, and we left downtown Ottawa. We found a quiet bar in the Glebe and drowned our sorrows till the ominous, doomy bell rang last call.

LISBON

We pulled into Lisbon at five and met Gomes, the promoter, at the venue. As he came up to the open driver's side window, you could smell the booze on his breath. It was a Saturday. We were a long way from the soothing Atlantic calm of the camp. Like climbing through a magical wardrobe to Narnia, on the other side of the van doors lay the tumultuous and pounding percussive pulse of Lisbon's wildlife carnival, taxicabs darting in and out of intersections, stray dogs barking on every corner, and long boulevards of illustrious hedonism punctuated by neon lights.

"How are you?"

"Good," Gomes answered. "Although I'm really tired. Been up all night. Big DJ party yesterday."

"So you haven't slept?"

"No," he replied, his eyes sunken into black circles on his tanned face. "Not at all."

We loaded in like a pack of exhausted dogs, down the long flights of stairs that went into the basement venue. The others went to the hotel to try and claim some sleep before the show, and by ten thirty Gomes had taken me to Bairro Alto and introduced me to some friends of his. The bartender, who of course he knew, free poured him what looked like half a pint of whiskey on the rocks.

Back at the venue, a fat old Portuguese man named Antonio was bartending, grey hairs poking through his sweaty shirt, unbuttoned a quarter down his chest, the physical embodiment of the smell of stale cologne.

Gomes went backstage to the greenroom, and I followed. There was a wall of lockers there, and when he opened his, he pulled out *Sabbath Bloody Sabbath* on CD. "It's the weekend, right?" he said. "You think I stay up all night drinking only coffee and booze?"

On the jewel case were four lines of pure white coke.

"Don't worry," he said. "It's from Peru."

Gomes railed a line and passed the coke to me.

"Don't tell anyone," he told me. "The owners of this place wouldn't like it."

I did a rip and passed back the jewel case with the coke and rolled bill. Almost on cue, Antonio stormed into the room and started yelling at Gomes in Portuguese. On his neck, a golden cross dangled from a chain and veins bulged with anger. Eventually, like a calming storm, the tension ceased, and Gomes offered him the CD case, where the roll and line lay crossed, both of his hands palm up like an altar boy begging for forgiveness. Antonio snorted a huge rail, Gomes forgiven.

After the show, I found Antonio behind the bar. He ushered me over and in broken English shouted into my ear over the throbbing bass of the DJ booth. "You know," I heard him say, "Gomes acts all special because he's been up for two days, but I've been up for two days too."

I laughed.

"Thing is," he said, while pouring me a beer. "I have twenty years on him."

Antonio cackled demonically, and the slow, intoxicating burn of the night continued from there. No one begins their night in Lisbon till at least midnight, so the band hadn't gone on till half past. At around two, the place had really started to fill with dancing, twisting bodies, all of them hands-raised and howling like wolves as the music pumped through the overhead speakers. I glanced over at Antonio, who looked frantic on the verge of heart attack, sweat dripping off the cross hanging from the gold chain, pouring beers behind the bar as the people streamed in. All of their jaws were clenched in the same all-night-all-morning frenzy as Gomes, all holding glasses as big as the whiskey he'd been poured in Bairro Alto earlier.

I turned back towards the DJ booth, and the men spinning records had just put on these huge horse masks, covering their entire heads. I was starting to really feel the booze and coke, and to me the DJs had completely transformed from human to horse. There were hairs growing from their pores and it was hooves, not four fingers and a thumb, that were choosing and spinning records. From beneath a hoof, with a sparkling horseshoe nailed to the bottom of it, the needle dropped, and the music's vibrations were felt across the shiny hardwood floor illuminated by the mirror ball that hung overhead.

They kept glancing back at each other, wordlessly talking about what record to pick next, which they'd fish for in their side bags and sometimes drop to the floor, but under the voluminous hum of the hard bass and powerful snares all I could see were their lips moving in "neighs" and "nahs" as the club erupted into torrential psychedelia.

A man and woman danced together to Blur's "Parklife" that effortlessly became "Isolation" by Joy Division—the horses at the booth nodding at each other in approval, then glancing back again at the turntables—before moving on to afrobeat and cuts from James Brown's *Live at the Apollo*. Their jaws chewed and chomped as though they were gnawing carrots with their teeth, then one of them pranced off towards the staff lockers backstage.

"Bem vindo a Lisboa!" Gomes yelled through the madness, coming up to me with massive black saucer eyes. Still holding his glass of whiskey, we got in his car and drove back up the hill to the Bairro Alto district. I left the band behind at the club, and Gomes and I alone prowled Lisbon's mad, bloodshot streets, drinking and yelling into a cavernous ecstasy. More barking dogs ran past us across the cobbled stones. Traffic honked and darted through the faintly starlit dark. Finally, the sun began to rise, and consciousness disappeared.

I woke up in the sweaty humidity of the van, damp and unclothed save for a pair of underwear, to the pounding force of the door opening. As I let out a tortured groan and rubbed the sleep from my eyes, still high and drunk from the night before, I rooted through my bag and took a quick inventory of my things.

The van pulled forward, eastward, towards Madrid.

EDMONTON

When we finally got back to Edmonton after the tour, Murky, Eoin, and Walter dropped me off at my parents' place. The watery blur of it all washed over me, and like a boxer the morning after a fight I sauntered drunkenly up the front walkway to the house.

My head hung low, and my hair was uncut and overgrown. I held my sleeping bag in one hand, my pillow under my arm, and I carried my guitar in the other hand. My bag swung from my shoulder. I felt like a mountain climber, reaching the top of some great summit as I set my things down in front of the door. I blinked slowly, exhausted, and rubbed my eyes.

As I pressed the doorbell, it all came back in a ringing instant—everything that had happened over the past few weeks flooding in like waves on the shores of my memories. Details, subtleties I'd forgotten: I was immersed in all of it, as time seemed to stand still, my body wading back and forth on a foamy, desolate beach.

Getting that first breath of the coming winter in Wisconsin while drinking whiskey from the bottle on a rooftop, all those kids my age in college towns asking me why I wasn't in school, successfully crossing the border illegally for the fourth tour in a row, the CN Tower coming into view as we drove into Toronto on the Don Valley Parkway, missing that exit in Montreal and screaming into the receiver of a roadside payphone to beg the promoter to bide us a few more minutes and push the show back, driving overnight to Thunder Bay and doing cocaine off the dashboard, hitting the prairies again and feeling that big flat land hit you like a smack of sobering cold water across the face, feeling so guilty for leaving Murk behind, and then that deer, that deer, the eye of that deer: it all came like gunfire in my mind, banging out like rounds of ammunition.

It felt like I had left another world—one that I might never have the chance to return to. The thought filled me with such terror, I started feeling sick and dizzy. I rubbed my eyes some more.

And then with a click of the latch my mom appeared at the door. She smiled, beaming from ear to ear, and gasped hello. As she opened up her arms, I turned to wave goodbye to the guys in the van, but they had already driven off, swallowed up by the late autumn prairie wind that picked up dirt loosed behind its rear wheels. Murk had sped off without even a honk of the horn, a cloud of blue smoke pluming from the exhaust.

I tried to comprehend how time could pass so fast and yet simultaneously so slow, and my mom's voice was almost unrecognizable—I think I answered with some shaky "hellos" as I gathered my things from the stoop and the memories of those nights continued pouring into me.

My mom wrapped her arms around me after what seemed like minutes, and so happily yelled, "Welcome home!" I dropped my bags as though my arms gave out and tried to worm my way out of her big bear hug.

"Mom," I said, quietly at first, trying to push her away. She only held me tighter. "Mom," I said again. "Mom, *fuck*!"

She backed off, a bit shocked, and a bit hurt.

"I'm happy to see you too," I said, sitting down on the chair in the hallway to untie my shoes. "Just give me a minute, though. Jesus."

She paused for a moment before walking silently back to the dining room table, where the book she was reading lay face down, spine bent. I picked my bags back up again with whatever strength I had left in me, lugged it all upstairs to my room, closed the door, and lay on my bed, staring up at the ceiling, alone with my pounding heart.

Eventually night fell and I went to brush my teeth, and through the bathroom door I could overhear my parents at the table. "He didn't even notice I made his bed," my mom said softly to my dad over the family dinner I'd opted out of. I doubt she knew I could hear her.

I opened the bathroom door quietly and turned off the light and crept back to my room. I lay wide awake for what seemed like hours: blinked slowly, exhausted, rubbed my eyes, and leapt from the bed towards my pile of unpacked things, unrolled the sleeping bag that had been thrown into the corner of the room, and slept on the floor.

The next morning, Murky called and told me he needed to talk. He was despondent by the time he pulled up in the van. His eyes were wet with tears, and he kept looking out the driver's side window, as though he was trying to figure out how to say something to me. He seemed like he was treading some fine line between trembling completely and holding it together.

"Murk," I said, reaching out to him, putting my hand on his shoulder. "What's up?"

He jolted away. "Don't," he said, raising his right hand. "Don't fucking touch me, man."

There was what seemed like a long pause.

"Why the fuck did you leave us there?" He asked me, his eyes widening. I could smell booze on his breath. "Why the fuck did you guys just turn your back? Why didn't you stay?"

I struggled to find the words. "I thought it was the most sensible thing, you know? I mean, think about what Eoin was saying, he was—"

"Sensible." He cut me off. He laughed once, quickly. "You know, Eoin told me what you talked about, in that truck to Toronto. Your *career*?"

I took that in. It made so much sense all of a sudden. Eoin needed them, Murky and Walter: he needed them to drive the van, he needed them to book the shows, to play his songs, to hold him up. And for that whole time, while we were together on the side of the 402 with our thumbs out, while we were together in the back of that truck heading to Pearson, he needed me to take the fall so he could keep them around.

"The way you turned your back, you know how that felt?" Murky said, looking away again, out the window, before his head jolted back. "I persuaded—*demanded* you join the band. They didn't want you around. I vouched for you so hard. So *fucking* hard. And you just left me there."

I started talking nervously: about how Eoin and I were both guitarists, about how we could pull the songs off with just the two of us, how the songs would come across with two vocalists and two acoustic guitars and we could still represent the records that way and . . .

"Fuck that," Murky said. "We're supposed to be a band. Your *career*? How about what matters more than that? Our friendship, everything we've done together? What we've been through?" Murk rubbed his eyes, wiping away exhaustion or tears, or both, before continuing.

"It was useless with Walter there. I did all that work myself. Found the bar, found the beds, found the van. He gave up the minute you guys left. I really could've used you. And instead you turned your fucking back on me and walked off like a coward. I needed you there."

There was another long, awkward silence. I looked forward through the windshield.

"I've known Eoin for longer than you can even know, man." He turned on the stereo. The Replacements were playing. "I know he's narcissistic. I know he's an opportunist. He's a fucking *songwriter*. I get all that."

He paused again, letting the music play for what seemed like forever.

"But you and I? We saved ourselves from drowning, remember?"

Murky turned the keys in the ignition. The van started up.

"Look, the guys and I talked. We can't afford to have another mouth to feed on the road. We tried to make it work, for a long time—but we've lost so much money on the last few tours, we don't know how we can keep bringing you. We have to trim the fat. And regardless, you don't even come close to having the stripes to decide if I'm the one who goes or gets left behind."

He reached across me and opened the passenger side door. "Now get the fuck out of the van."

MADRID

We got to Madrid after a seven-hour drive in the massive Sprinter van that nearly took up the entire width of the narrow, crowded streets of the Spanish capital. Davey's hands clutched the wheel and his knuckles were white when we entered the madness of the city, its barrage of traffic sending up swirls of multilingual profanity that takes on its own momentum. We would move forward ten metres, then sit gridlocked for ten minutes, then move forward, then repeat, until we found the venue and loaded in, late and without sound check.

Davey was pale and exhausted from the drive. The cataclysmic partying of Lisbon, the three-day sprint from London to Portugal, and the red-eye flight that got him there had all compounded. He was driving every mile, since he refused to let anyone else take the wheel. It was his band, he always said, so the driver's seat was also *his* in the van.

It was a typical Sunday show; attendance was sparse, to say the least. Backstage we looked at each other as pools of sweat formed underneath us in the sweltering room. Although dark outside, the Iberian heat clutched us tight from waking to sleeping, and there seemed to be no escape from the messy, dripping weather.

After the show, it was even worse, ripping off our shirts and throwing them into the steaming pile that had already formed in a corner backstage. Then we sit, sweating, with our heads in our hands, staring as the beads drop on the floor.

We plowed through the load-out at full speed, desperately trying to get it done. By three or four shows, we'd had the pack down to a science. But it never seemed to get any easier.

"Speaker cabinets!" Davey yelled, standing atop the tail of the van, perched in the trunk, arm outstretched, directing the load-out's proverbial traffic. He was still wearing that denim jacket, and his sunglasses were still on his head, despite the punishing heat of the Spanish night. His jacket collar was raised, and its sleeves were rolled up to his forearms. Beneath the thick denim, you could see the sweat soaking through his shirt. "Cabinets first, then drum shells, amp heads next. Guitars on top. That's our pack, come on! Let's *go!*"

Harrison and I pushed road cases at a near sprint, stacked six feet high with drums and guitars, over bumps and around corners in the club as Spanish shooter girls stopped us in our tracks to pour test tubes of ice-cold Jägermeister down our throats. We shook our heads the way a dog dries off, and then pushed forward, out the door.

"This club's got a curfew of eleven thirty, guys," Davey continued, lifting guitar cases up inside the back of the van. At one point Harrison stopped, keeled over, the Spanish heat dripping off of his face. "Stop sucking wind, Harry, let's go! We gotta move, come on!"

Hot Snakes, Black Flag, the Germs, or something of equal speed and volume was probably playing loudly on the van stereo as Gerry gathered up the merch inside. Almost on cue, as soon as he threw the last LP in a cardboard box, I swooped in and snatched it up, the last thing on top of that mountain of gear and guitars that was piled up in the back of the Sprinter.

"Okay, we good?" Davey said, slamming the door. "Dummy check? Harrison, you on it?"

"Yup," and he ran inside, full tilt, phone light on, scanning the ground for any cables, picks, strings, or shrapnel that might have fallen to the floor. "We're good! Let's go!"

Davey, already settled with the promoter, pressed on the gas while the back door was still open, and Harrison leapt in, slamming it shut behind him. As we pulled out into the fully charged Madrid traffic that practically spiralled out of control, we surveyed each other, drenched in sweat, through the darkness of the van.

There wasn't even a point in trying to estimate how many times in the past I'd done that: how many load-outs lay in my wake, and how many more were yet to come. The numbers were unfathomable. All I knew was that I was in the middle of a whirlpool of a ride. As Davey drove through the streets of Madrid towards the hotel, we all sat silent and gazed out different windows from our places in the van.

The sticky sweat that drenched our clothes also caused the dim urban light to reflect off our skin. Harrison peeled the shirt off his back, crumpling it into a small, sweaty ball. He looked around for a replacement.

"Anybody seen my Hot Water Music shirt?" Harrison said, taking out his phone to shine his light on the spotless floor. "It was here a minute ago . . . Fuck sakes, how do I keep losing shit?"

Davey stayed silent, focussed on the road. He had these big dark circles around his exhausted eyes, and there were grey hairs growing in the thickness of his unshaven, gnarly beard. As I noticed how Davey was really finally starting to show his age, I thought back to my first few tours, and the distance of time and space that separated the now from then.

There I was: back in a small Ford Windstar, a far humble cry from the towering Sprinter that I now called home. I had these waves of memory envelope me like the ocean had only a few days before. I was swirling in it, this washing machine: the past and the present seemed to come to a grinding halt in that single moment, like a driver pounding on the brakes of a tour van, screeching to a stop on the highway. All of it came back to me, all at once. All of it.

In a rush, I remembered all the hardwood floors, the lack of sleep and food, and the dismal, tragic end to those relationships I'd forged in that doomed Windstar. In comparison, the tall blue Sprinter with its immaculately clean interior dwarfed that beat up old Ford minivan. But still, as we quietly and slowly moved through Madrid, I closed my eyes and thought back to a very different time and place, eighteen years old, the frontiers of touring still so mysterious and exciting.

RIDING THE DOG

A few days later I decided I was moving to Toronto. I was going to just up and leave, that was it. No band, no job, no university degree: there was nothing left for me in Edmonton. I was done and I was flat broke. I couldn't afford a flight, so I went to the Greyhound station across the street from the Grand Hotel and the massive dirt parking lot next to MacEwan University and bought a ticket to Toronto for a hundred dollars.

My dad dropped me off around eleven thirty at night. There was a sadness written in the lines of age on his face that day, as a group of three men shared a bottle of Royal Reserve by the main doors while another slammed the door of a locker just inside the station for eating his last few bits of change. Most people gathering around the bus gate had their belongings in plastic bags. This is how the masses travel: on a bus adorned with the image of a skinny, underfed grey dog. The few clothes I had had been tossed in a duffel bag. The night was a solid black as more unsavoury characters that claimed a home on the streets of downtown Edmonton circled the depot like vultures on a drying bone.

"I'll see ya," I said to my dad from the passenger seat, and some reluctant tears began to well up in his eyes as he saw me off. I climbed aboard the bus that read *Toronto*, and it hissed before lurching forward into the wintry and unwelcoming void of the Canadian prairie.

The driver laid the schedule out to all of us through the distorted intercom system that he held up to his face like a lantern of hope. In a long list, as the bus veered left and merged onto Yellowhead Trail, he robotically read aloud the stops the coach would make en route to its terminal destination in the Big Smoke.

"Lloydminster, Battleford, Saskatoon, Yorkton, Brandon, Winnipeg, Kenora, Dryden, Upsala, Thunder Bay, Sudbury, Barrie, and finally," and then with a kind of subdued pause, and a small squelch of shrill mic feedback, like an exhale, he said: "Toronto."

He had another pause, while Edmonton blurrily sped by through the windows of the bus. "Thank you for choosing Greyhound, enjoy your journey with us today."

The bus lights went off. People tried to get comfortable, turning and writhing in their seats in desperate attempts to sleep through the overnight trip to Saskatoon. Right then, the distance ahead hit me. I felt around in my pocket for the last few bills I had, probably about 130 bucks, double-checking it was still there. I found my ticket, rubbed my eyes a little, unfolded it from the pocket of my coat and re-read the names of the cities and towns that had just been broadcast over the bus's loudspeaker. The driver faintly turned up the radio, broadcasting that nineties song that had come on in the van right before we hit the deer. I struggled again, to think of what band it was, and in my mind I replayed Murk, Eoin, and Walter arguing over that bottle of liquor about their name, that long-forgotten Vancouver band who'd faded into Canadian rock obscurity, now existing only on the static of the airwaves.

In my mind, I drew a line east along Highway 16, connecting with the Trans-Canada in Manitoba somewhere, that wound its way above the Great Lakes before snaking its way down through Northern Ontario, dropping dead at the lakeshore a few blocks south of Dundas and Bay. I wondered how many people in how many other bands who had driven that route had just faded away, like a radio station when you leave the city. The song ended, and eventually we were outside of broadcast radius. The driver turned off the radio and the bus fell silent.

I shut my eyes to try to sleep, or to comprehend all that distance that lay before me, the names of the towns we'd stop in made tiny little dots appear on the great empty space of the map in my mind. Passengers would leave and board like flies through the air of a kitchen in summer, and the bus would continuously pull forward, its steel frame forgetting them completely. And all that lay between these tiny places was an unpopulated, vast and sprawling plain, its green and dying grass blowing horizontal in the might of the wind, and I rode wordlessly for days beneath a blanket of endless sky.

The farther east we got, the farther it seemed we had to go. The sun rose and fell and the wheels obediently turned and turned, perpetually carrying us through time and space, like ghosts passing through a long and forgotten dream.

AUTOBAHN

We had all just gotten off the stage in Leipzig and we were driving to Dresden to spend the night. We talked about Portugal, about Spain, about France, the warm hospitality of Europeans and the incredible food and drink, the ease with which you could score weed and hash, and the freedom and beauty of living your life how you and only you intended: in a maelstrom, a torrential downpour, of music.

"Beats Canada, hey?" I asked him, gesturing at the road ahead. "The winters, long drives, getting treated like shit . . ."

"Yeah, no kidding," he said. "You know, this one time? I was playing in Hamilton, and the band shows up, and it was, like, this corporate event, right? And so, given that the gig's in a steakhouse, we asked the promoter if we'd be able to have a meal." Davey signalled and merged onto the road after the exit for Dresden and then continued. "And the guy sighs, looks around, and hesitantly goes, 'Yeah, yeah. I'll order you a pizza.' So a few hours go by, we load in—up two flights of stairs, of course—sound check, and then after we're done, we ask him where the pizza is."

It was the dead of night, so Davey pressed on the gas.

"And he takes us to this tiny little room where there's, like, the smallest fucking pizza you've ever seen, sitting on top of this deep freeze. So, with him standing there, and us looking back at him kind of in disbelief, we open the box. Hey—" he interrupted himself, handing me his weed and a magazine, "can you roll a joint?"

I started busting up the nugs and he went on.

"So, yeah, we open the box, and then all of a sudden buddy goes, 'Whoa, whoa, *no*. You can't eat in here.' So we go, 'Okay . . . where's the greenroom?' And he takes us through the crowd that's forming—a big crowd. And with this little fucking box of pizza, we're following him behind the bar, and guess where he takes us?"

I shook my head.

"The fucking broom closet."

I laughed.

All Canadian musicians have a similar story. You drive six to eight hours, across the frozen lowlands of the prairies, or the desolate rocky Shield of Northern Ontario, and even if you pack a place, the staff still treat you like a nuisance. At times it feels like there's no ceiling to the amount of money you can bring into a bar as a touring band in Canada and not be treated like shit. The standard Canadian guarantee for an independent band is four drink tickets before you start your set and a boot out the door when you're done.

Europe for me seemed so much more civilized. Even in the UK, where you couldn't necessarily get more free beer just by asking for it—not in the way you could in Germany, Belgium, or the Czech Republic, where it flowed in what seemed like a limitless supply—but at least you'd be allowed to bring your own into the greenroom. Even a compromise was better than Canada's draconian laws about booze, where it already seemed like you'd be getting screwed as a musician some way or another no matter what.

We exchanged stories about Canada for ages that night. I told him a few about the early days, with Murky and Eoin and Walter. He talked about driving eight hours from Winnipeg to Saskatoon and finding out day-of that the bar had been repossessed by bikers, so the show was cancelled. We both had a similar story about driving from Edmonton to Vancouver through the Rockies in the winter only to finally get to Vancouver and have no one come to see you on a Tuesday night except the owner's dog and the bar staff. I remembered once taking the ferry from Vancouver to Victoria under the pretense that the ticket would be covered by the promoter and then going to settle with him after the show, receipt in hand, and having him nowhere to be found and his phone going straight to voicemail.

We laughed in the sadness of it all, both looking out the windshield as the lines whizzed by, wondering if it was determination or insanity that propelled us to continue. But regardless of motivation, those times are what define you. Through all of them, great moments were had, and most of them make you either even more determined or tremendously more insane.

"What's the greatest show you've ever played?" I asked him as we sparked the joint.

He thought for a second.

"Probably in Halifax, early nineties. It was this terrible winter, dead of January, snowstorms were nonstop that whole trip. We got to the show almost four hours late because of the weather, gridlocked on the highway, and we show up *right* as we're supposed to go on, load in through this packed, sweaty, sold-out room of people—right through the people, onto the stage, set up, and *bang!*"—he motioned with his hand—"the room fucking *exploded*."

He described the way in which the Maritime audience lost their shit: climbing on the rafters, jumping onstage to share the mic, knowing every word, pogoing like maniacs, dancing with each other, a downpour of sweat and fire, long hair in every direction, one of those total mythological blurs of humanity, the kind of gig you play only once in every hundred.

All of that, with the day leading up to it—the horrible drive, the terrible weather, the under-heated van, the broken radiator, the shitty, nervous load-in, the lack of sound check— at the end of that long dark tunnel of a day on the road, was a powerful and luminescent light.

He paused again.

"Fuck, man. That was the *best* band."

Davey looked out the windshield longingly, and I could see his eyes, red from the dope, well up a bit with tears. It seemed like a long pause, silence in the van save for the sound of the wheels churning and grinding out beneath us.

"What happened?" I asked, as he passed me the joint.

"We suffered the fate of all bands," Davey said, smiling coyly for just a second. "We broke up."

"How?" I inhaled. "Why?"

"Well," Davey said, putting on his indicator to pass another vehicle, like us, trudging along the highway at night. "I fucked the singer's girlfriend."

Totally caught off guard, I coughed; a few shocked laughs in between the clouds of smoke billowing out of me. "What?"

"Yeah. Quite the story," he remarked casually, then began. "I was living in Vancouver at the time. Totally different city: it was so fuckin' cheap back then," he said, reaching for the rest of the spliff, which was now just a small, burnt piece of rolling paper clinging to the filter. Davey rolled the window down and threw it out, its ember drawing a thin orange line through the air as it raced backwards behind the van.

"We were doing alright. A lot of support from the local radio station. We were getting great shows, we were drawing. You remember Richard's on Richards?"

I nodded.

"Well, that was like our home turf. We were selling it out pretty consistently. Our tours were doing really well. The usual bullshit: label interest, agents flying in to see us play, that typical music industry jack-off routine. We had this song, it got played on the radio in the nineties a ton."

Davey sang one of the lines, humming the lead guitar part. I immediately recognized it: the song that played when Eoin, Murk, Walter, and I had hit the deer in Michigan a few years ago, the song that played on the Greyhound bus when I was heading to Toronto. I couldn't believe I was hearing it again, here and now, and had never made the connection before. I laughed a bit, melancholically.

"Anyways." Davey sighed, his eyes fixed on the road. "The singer got all fucking smarmy all of a sudden. It was like it was overnight. Didn't want to play any more of my songs, started writing my parts for me, all that garbage. We started butting heads, rehearsals got more infrequent, and if they even happened, they usually ended kind of badly. But the shows kept selling out."

He wrung at the steering wheel with his hands, like his palms were getting sweaty.

"I was pretty good friends with him and the girl he was dating. She and I actually used to go out for beers, you know? She'd tell me about how he was starting to get all cocky and narcissistic at home too. The little bit of success really changed him."

Through some snores in the back seat we heard a cough, some tossing and turning. I rolled the window up.

"So," Davey said, with a glance over at me, "we signed a record deal. And this one night, she came over, when I knew everyone else was going out to this label party to celebrate, and we started going at it. And who busted into the room, a few hours later?"

My eyebrows raised. "No."

"You bet," Davey said, laughing. "We got in this huge fight: she was screaming, we were throwing punches, breaking plates, all that shit. We ended up going to court. They ended their relationship and the band broke up. I got that fucker clean back for all his bullshit. No more fucking telling me what to play and when to play it. I went my own way, moved out east to Toronto, started playing my own songs. I regret fucking *nothing*."

We were silent again for just a moment.

"Man, but some of those shows . . ." He shook his head, trailing off nostalgically. "They're worth it," Davey said, inhaling. "The haul, I mean. The load-in, the drive, the sound check; it's all worth it if the show is great. Canada wears you down because, so often, the shows are so bad. You get treated like shit. Nobody comes. Nobody promotes. You get screwed out of money. We all know the stories; they've happened to all of us. But, when it's *worth* it?"

Exhale.

"It's the best feeling in the world." Davey rolled up the sleeves and popped the collar of his freshly washed, immaculately pressed jean jacket. "I'll do whatever it takes for that feeling. Whatever it fucking takes."

Davey and I sat in quiet contemplation, before I suggested putting the Replacements on the stereo. "No thanks," he said, right before he pointed at a bulge of crumpled black fabric on the dashboard. "Fucking hate that band. Hey, man, can you pass me Harrison's fucking gross, sweaty shirt?" I grabbed it off the dash and handed it to him. "Thanks, man. I also hate when shit lies around in the van. I swear to god the AC is blowing his fucking smell everywhere. Drives me crazy."

Davey threw the shirt over his shoulder, and it landed across Harrison's face. "Put your shit in your bag, Harry," Davey yelled, before retreating back to total silence. The white lines of the German highway raged beneath us as we pulled into Dresden and stocked up on sleep for the journey to west Germany in the morning.

PRAGUE

"Those nationalist idiots," spat a man over the bar-room roar of a pub in Žižkov, Prague 3. He had long black dreaded hair, and he was quickly rolling joints as long and skinny as his boney fingers. "It's happening all over Europe right now. Do they have any idea how stupid they all sound?"

The crumple of paper and tobacco as it was touched by lighter flame was inaudible in the din. As he took his first drag, he held out the hand holding the Zippo, index finger stretched out towards me, only to prove his point.

"They say, 'My mother was a Croat, my father was a Serb, my grandfather was Hungarian, but *I*...'" and he gazed through me, as though at a ghost in the bar, with condemning eyes, "'*I, I* am *Czech*.'"

He took a hit from his spliff and raged on, and on. Instead of security circling him, or bouncers pouncing, his voice only grew louder beneath the curved and arched ceilings of the bar that was a former military bunker. He kept paying for his drinks, and so the bartender kept serving, and the other patrons left. Those that remained thought nothing much of it. He was just a man yelling about freedom in the corner of an empty bar that refused to stop serving him. Another day in Prague.

A tiny bead of spit formed on his bottom lip and I got up to leave the bar. "*When* will the history of Europe not be the history of *fighting in* Europe?" I could still hear him yelling as I wandered out onto the street and tried to figure out what tram to take back to the hotel. His drunken words echoed through the streets of the Czech capital.

When I finally found my way back, I sat down on the hotel bed, next to Gerry, and put my head into my palms. I'd been drinking so much all night, smoking constantly. I could feel the wear and tear this tour was raging on my body. A feeling of anxiety washed over me, distant at first, then coming in waves.

"I feel like I can't even *breathe*," I said. "Is it the smoke? Is it the booze?"

Gerry switched off the hotel room light and turned over on his side, a mumbled exhausted tone coming out of his mouth. I saw three Pilsner Urquell bottles on his bedside table—two of them empty—and assumed that he'd been out in the streets of Prague earlier too. "There's no point trying to struggle. You can't fight the ocean, the ocean will always win."

Gerry almost immediately fell back asleep. *That's the first thing I've heard him say in days*, I thought, staring up at the ceiling, wide awake, my heart and thoughts racing. *We all have our vices, I suppose, and I guess that's how he copes: silence and sleep.*

I couldn't sit still. I grabbed one of the beers and left the hostel to wander up and down that great big hill in Žižkov that leads to the television tower, with all those grey baby aliens crawling along its side up towards the sky. I used it like a North Star, a guiding light through the darkness of night, as I sucked that bottle of Czech pilsner dry.

Out of the darkness I heard a "Holy shit!" and turned my head, almost dropping my bottle to the ground. "What the fuck are you doing here?" the voice yelled.

There she was: Breigh, a longtime friend from my years in Edmonton, who would frequent the parties that Murky and Eoin would throw at their house on University Avenue before and after our long, intoxicated US tours. I was completely shocked to see her. She ran up to me, and at first I barely recognized her. After a while, you realize a person can have this way of looking so different over the years—not just hair and clothes and weight, but physical and emotional maturity, a comportment we all develop in some way or another, hopefully—but yet also somehow look very much the same.

The odds were next to impossible that I would've run into anyone I knew in Prague, let alone someone from Edmonton. But Breigh was on a backpacking trip across Europe, heading to Germany to spend some time in Leipzig—"Leipzig," I said, my voice echoing off the derelict graffiti-covered communist apartments, "my favourite city in Germany,"—and then we tore off down the street together. In that random, magical moment, all the years, all the memories, all the laughs and tears caught up to us with the force of a semitrailer, barrelling towards the present.

Sitting in a bar, I told her about the tour, about how there was only a week left, about how long I'd been out, and about how it always seemed like what were endless, endless miles of

highway were somehow rushing to an end despite the fact that a new tour was just beginning and the cycle would begin again.

"And what about you?"

At once it all came tumbling out, those years in Edmonton and moving away. And going to school, and moving to Vancouver, and the Emily Carr University of Art + Design, and leaving friends behind, and what was going on with Murky, and Eoin, and Walter.

"What?" I stopped her short. "You still talk to them?"

She was silent for just a second. "So, you didn't hear?"

I shook my head, and she began.

"They all moved east," she said, "to Montreal, not long after that last tour you did with them, where you guys parted ways. Without any goodbyes, they left. Packed up the amps, bailed on their rent, didn't even phone their moms, it was so sudden—just like that, across the Trans-Canada, playing shows along the way."

As the months turned into years, the drinking got worse; as the drinking got worse, the shows got smaller. The promoters stopped booking them, the songs stopped getting written, Walter stopped going to practices. Someone got a phone call in Edmonton, saying the band had broken up, that Eoin was headed back home—hitchhiking, maybe, though someone said he'd sold his guitar for a Greyhound ticket—but Murky stayed in Montreal.

"Last I heard," she said, her voice getting really quiet, "Murky was living in an apartment on Peel . . . some friends of mine said that he started using heroin."

As she told the story, I could picture it clear as day: One burning hot Montreal summer evening, there was Murky, cooking his smack with a spoon over a lighter, biting that rubber around his left arm as the veins swelled, plunging in that needle like a firefighter swallowed by the forest igniting. And then, hours later, he came to, paralyzed, save for the right side of his body, which pulled him down the stairs of his apartment, out the front door as the sun rose, and towards Montreal General. That right arm of his pulled him across Avenue des Pins as the traffic whizzed by, dodging and swerving. He pulled himself with that same arm into the emergency room.

"The worst part?" She asked, before swallowing and clearing her throat. "He was so constipated from the heroin, but, you know, he had that spoon, right?"

I nodded.

"He managed somehow to pull himself, with that same right arm, into the bathroom in the hospital, and dig the shit out of his own ass."

I was silent.

That spoon, I could only think, though I thought I'd said it out loud. That cooked spoon: the same spoon that dug him into that deep, dark pit was the same spoon that dug him out. Of course, that could only ever happen to Murky, and his determined, headstrong, and otherworldly obsession with never failing, carrying every amp, finishing every bottle, whether or not it would be to the very dark and bitter end.

She shook her head, looking out the window teary-eyed, wondering how I'd never heard the story. The painstaking determination of his addictions had finally gotten the better of him. His band had split up, he was broke, and he had long since hit the bottom, but still, he would not lose.

"After that," she continued, "he kicked the habit, got better. Not really sure what he's doing now."

LONDON

After Prague, we headed west towards Brussels, via Nuremberg, Frankfurt, and Cologne. I couldn't quite believe it, but the tour was ending. There I was, on that beach in Portugal, what seemed like only minutes ago, staring out into that overwhelming mass of water that surrounded me.

The plan was to hit Calais after Brussels and tackle the border first thing in the morning so we could make our flights to London then home the following night. Davey couldn't shut up about his week in London, in meetings with labels, with agents, with music industry bigwigs; that's where Davey was in his element. Every time he popped the collar of that immaculate jean jacket as he drove the van, in his mind he was going over every single way he was going to try to sell himself and his new record to those execs in their ivory tower.

Davey pulled the van up to the Brussels venue at five thirty and the door was open. Freddie, our sound guy that night, was inside, setting up the mics. There was that unspoken sadness between all of us, the last show of the tour, this strange, unique emotional cocktail of satisfaction, pride, relief, and unmitigated despair. No one was talking much. Clocks were being watched. Everybody sat around the venue, heads buried in phones, messaging home: begging for a ride from the airport, lining up some work, or making plans to meet at the local bar.

Our show was great. Six weeks on the road together playing every night tightens you up, you start breathing together, no words get spoken, only nods and approving glances. We played our hearts out, the way you do on the final night. Not only are you playing the show like it's your last, but that's really the case, and so you leave it all on stage, cleansing yourself of those little resentments that only exist within the van. The entirety of the journey feels like it all comes down to this.

And then, that last chord. It rings out into the crowd as cheers subdue it, and you exit the stage, grab a towel, dry off backstage. The greenroom is a humid, steamy chamber. Some beers might be spilled, bottles lie now in tiny puddles on the floor. Your bag's still unzipped from when you grabbed from it earlier. You come to terms with the fact there's no show tomorrow, and all of a sudden time starts to slow down. You hit the present like it's a brick wall. All of the memories from the past six weeks come flooding back to you and everything seems so incredibly close yet so very far away.

"Alright, guys." Davey came through the door. "Let's load out, I guess."

The last load-out is always slower than all the ones before it. There's nowhere to get to, so you take your time. The lid of the road case casually snaps against the bottom, and your guitar is nicely tucked away, not thrown in with haste and dominance. It's just a travel companion now; soon you'll see it on the conveyor belt at oversized luggage, and in your mind you'll silently wish it goodbye as it's whisked away. You'll need it again when you set out on your next tour. The only real break from the madness is the very end.

The bar gradually clears. Everything goes into the back of the van and the doors shut, one last time, on that equipment. At that moment, with that loud and profound clunk, load-out exists to you no more.

"Hey, man," Davey called out to me. "Great tour."

I put out my hand and he shook it. "You too."

We all stood there, laughing, smoking, for a few minutes. There were a few seconds of silence, then someone cracked a can of beer, and the three of us got lost in conversation, reflecting about the past few weeks. Harrison and I laughed about drinking in Portugal with those surfers, both of us wondering if it was purgatory or paradise they'd submitted their lives to. While Harrison was in the middle of telling a long and winding joke, Davey quietly snuck around to the van, where Freddie, now off the clock, was waiting in the dark. Davey handed him some cash and Freddie passed him a baggie. They shook hands, talked for a few more seconds, and as Freddie said goodbye, out of the corner of my eye I saw Davey pick up one or two of Harrison's sweaty, crumpled shirts from the back seat and walk them over to a trash can on the side of the street.

Holy fuck, I thought. *That's what he's been doing this whole time? Throwing out his clothes?*

Each bit of silence got longer than the last, and Davey finally came back into the circle, looking me dead in the eye, knowing that I saw the whole exchange, from start to finish. A look in his face told me to keep my mouth shut, though it was far too late to say anything to him anyway. My eyes moved from his to a choice spot on the ground. I tapped my foot, anxious and awkward. Murky, Eoin, or even Walter, despite their short-comings, never would've gone behind anybody's back like that, sneaking around the van, exerting silent dominance, casually disposing of someone else's things whenever it suited them, and secretly buying drugs. I kept one hand in my pocket. The other clutched an almost-empty can of beer, so tight with anger it was denting the sides. Two pulls left, maybe.

Then it set in that our time was up. Best get on with reality, walk back through that rabbit hole after the plane lands and lead a normal life. There's no easy way to deal with it, so just bite the bullet and get back home. Everyone piled into the van, and we pulled out of Brussels, headed towards the French coast. I shut my eyes, for what seemed like just a moment. When they opened again, we were in queue in Calais to cross back into the UK.

I rubbed my eyes a little. Realized I hadn't given my bag one last run-through to make sure there wasn't anything I forgot to toss out: hash, or weed, or worse. I knew Davey had a sack on him, and I didn't want to risk us getting busted any more than we already were.

"Davey," I said, leaning forward from the back. "Fuck, man—I didn't check my bag. Totally forgot to give it a once-through. We threw out all the hash, right?"

Davey laughed. "I think it'll be fine," he said. "They're just going to wave us through again. Don't worry, in all my years, I've never been caught."

"Fuck, it's just one of those things, man, you can't fuck with a border like that." I leaned back in my chair, not totally convinced he'd gotten the message. In my mind, I pictured him pulling over, coming to his senses, throwing out whatever it was that Freddie had sold him. Davey turned around in his chair, black rings around his stoned, dehydrated, exhausted eyes.

"Seriously, dude," he said to me, his tone suddenly sharp and controlling. "Don't worry. Be fucking cool."

Gerry woke up, too, with a stretch. "Are we already here?" he asked, yawning.

Davey didn't answer, just pulled the car forward through the line as cars got waved through. He put on his sunglasses. To this day I'm not sure why I didn't call him out, right then and there. I could swear the van stunk of hash and weed, and I thought of all the agents, promoters, managers, and music industry execs that Davey would try to win over by showing off a heaping sack. I pictured him wandering around London, stoned out of his mind, all our careers worth the risk so he could have his own stash for a week. My heart was racing and I was fucking livid.

We finally pulled up to the window, and I could feel the beads of sweat start to form on my forehead. We had to wait for a minute while the border guards changed shifts. As one stood up, the other sat down in his swivel chair, logging in to the computer, starting his day. He slid open the window and leaned out into the morning sun.

"Hello, mate," he said, "how are you doing today?"

"Tired!" Davey said, totally keeping his cool, as he lit a smoke. He still had his sunglasses on. "Drove overnight from a gig in Belgium."

"You're a band?" the border guard asked. "Any gigs in the UK? You got your Certificates of Sponsorship?"

"We're actually flying out of Heathrow this evening," Davey said, reaching for the stack of passports on the dashboard. "We just finished our tour. We were in the UK a few weeks ago."

"Alright then, let's see those passports." He took them from Davey's hand and glanced through them before closing the window. "I assume you're David, yes? And that's Gerald, beside you in the passenger seat?"

"Gerry," Davey corrected him. "We call him Gerry."

"Okay, great. You mind opening the side doors so I can have a look at everyone else?"

I nudged Harrison in the side so he could wake up and give a quick wave to the guard. A few seconds passed, though to me they seemed like hours. Harrison had reclined in his seat, his eyes closed, letting out a yawn.

I expected the worst: I was sure we'd be directed to the next office and searched, and they'd find whatever it was Davey was hiding in the glove compartment.

The window slid open again and he passed the passports back to Davey. "All looks good, mate," he said. "Have a safe flight home."

We drove off through Dover and hit the A20 towards London. After a few minutes, Davey opened the glove box, laughing with his fist in the air, whooping and hollering. He handed me his papers and a sack of weed. Inside was a flap of coke. "Mind rolling a joint there, bud?"

I shook my head and looked out the window. "What the fuck was that?" I spat. "Have you lost your fuckin' mind?"

Davey glanced at me in the rear-view mirror, changing sights between me and the road. "What the fuck are you talking about," he said, without the inflection of a question. "Are you the one that stayed up all night driving? We've still got to make it to the airport, after we drop off this gear. You think I'm going to do all that without getting high?"

"Yeah, dude," I said, angrily. "I do. What the fuck do you think I'm going to say? You could've fucked us all so hard back there. *You're* the one who insists on doing all the driving. *You're* the one with enough shit on you to get us all arrested, not to mention banned from the UK forever."

Davey laughed again. "As if you haven't been getting high this whole time," he said. "Suddenly you want to play babysitter?"

The argument woke Harrison. "What's wrong," he said, with an exhausted sigh.

"He's mad because we snuck this dope across the border," Davey said, rolling a joint with his hands anchored in the middle of the wheel. "After that whole tour, hitting my stash, and now suddenly he doesn't want to celebrate." Harrison shrugged and went back to sleep. Gerry had been out cold the whole time. It was Davey and I alone, staring each other down in the mirror. Through his sunglasses I could tell his red stoned eyes were fixed right on me.

"Fuckin' hypocrite," he said, holding the steering wheel with his knees as he gave the joint a final twist, put it between his lips, and lit it. "You don't like it, you can fuckin' leave. There's a long line of bored Canadian kids that want to be outta their minds playing guitar for me in Europe."

I felt as though a thousand pounds of water had just fallen on me, crushing. I was so mad it was hard to breathe, trapped inside the vehicle, as it raced north.

That whole day in London was gruelling. We spent hours navigating rush hour traffic in the morning, white knuckling it as we inched forward through the city, seeing the numbers on the clock inch closer and closer to our check-in time at Heathrow.

I sat fuming in the back, exhausted and angry, wondering why after everything we'd been through together somebody would throw it all on the line like that.

When we got to the backline company's warehouse, I silently helped everyone unload the gear, as they laughed and joked, gathering around the front of the van to hit some more of the drugs Davey had arrogantly snuck into England. I just climbed into the back seat and closed the door.

"Someone pissed in his cornflakes this morning," I heard Davey say. Everybody got in, and we headed to Heathrow. I wanted so bad to open my mouth and bring Davey into the spotlight, come clean with the truth about why and how all of Harrison's clothes had gone missing. But there was no point, I thought: this was it for me.

A driver from the rental company met us at the airport and we handed off the keys, giving the van a last-minute once-over, checking to see if there was anything we'd buried and forgotten beneath the equipment over the past month and a half: empty bottles, abandoned underwear, gifted CDs or seven-inch records, unopened packs of guitar strings.

Davey took me aside before I went through security.

"So," he said, "are we cool?"

"No, man," I answered. "We're not. That was so fucking stupid. I can't believe you'd do that, put everyone's career at risk like that—"

"*Career?*" he leaned in closer to me. "Grow the fuck up. *I'm* your career."

I stared him down. We both stood silent, for what seemed like forever, before Davey continued.

"Nothing was going to happen. They didn't look through the van, they never do. In all my years, it's never happened. It's not the States. And anyway," Davey said, with a slight arrogant sigh. "When you're in my band, it goes my way. I'm the one who wanted to bring you along. I'm the one who hired you. This is your golden ticket. If you don't like it, then you can go the same way as Harrison's dirty, fuckin' shitty clothes."

Fuming, I walked towards the gate to get in line, and as the boarding call went out over the speakers of Heathrow, I turned to watch Davey, pushing fifty, adjust the collar and sleeves of his prized jean jacket one last time, desperate for an avenue to stay relevant.

As Davey said goodbye to everybody and walked towards the Tube station to head to London, I walked through security and got on the plane, without uttering a word the entire way.

Before even a single thought of what I'd say to Davey the next time I saw him—in a bar in Toronto, or on the street, or at a show—I thought of the crowds and lights, unsure if it was a dream, a memory, or a premonition. They always cheer so loudly, and the louder they cheer, the brighter the lights shine, at least to you. After the crowds leave and the lights go off, you come home, and everything is quiet and dark. You wonder how you'll adjust, and you can't reconnect.

NAUTICAL DISASTER AGAIN

My thoughts tumbled over and over upon themselves on the long subway ride home from Pearson.
I hadn't slept on the flight and barely said goodbye
to everyone when I landed. I kept thinking of the
feeling of being in that van with Murky, and how
I'd given it up. He and Eoin were unpredictable,
careless, and their addictions had consumed them,
but at least I could trust them. Everything I'd been
through with Davey had all become meaningless.

What's next? I kept asking myself. *What am I going
to do besides tour?* A college dropout, the moving wall
of thirty barrelling towards me at the speed of passing
time, with barely any job experience and no money in
the bank. All those tours that could be coming my
way, all those paid gigs, recording sessions, all those
dreams that I'd had: I'd wind up the same as Davey,

pushing fifty with barely an earthly possession other than a lunatic amount of pride.

"Don't make life decisions when you're drunk and insane. Don't make life decisions when you're drunk and insane," I repeated. "And above all, finish the tour."

I decided that I had to spend some nights at my girlfriend's cottage up north to dry out. The thirst for booze was desperately strong and the dreams that whole week were terrible: By the second night, I was back in the washing machine, being thrown and tossed around by the waves, readying myself to drown. By the third, I was trapped in a van, nowhere to run, surrounded by three Daveys, all of them showing off their own sack of weed as the border approached. On night four I was out in the middle of Lake Michigan, pulling Murky up and out of the waves. On the fifth night, I was back on the beach, looking out into that vast, overwhelming ocean. By the end of the week, I was getting the Greyhound back to the city, with a quick stop in Kitchener to change buses.

The Toronto Maple Leafs were broadcast in silence from an old television set that hung above the jaundiced skin and knotty elbows of five middle-aged patrons who sat at the bar in the Kitchener bus station on Thanksgiving night. These lone men found a macabre solace amidst the alcoholics and sports fans congregating round their substitute for a turkey dinner with family: the frosty tap connected to a keg of GLB lager that sold that night for $3.75 a pint.

"Do you want a large glass, or a small one?" the bartender asked as I fumbled for change in my pocket, looking out the windows of the station at the typical run-down urban fabric of Southwestern Ontario.

"Large," I replied, and gave her the cost plus tip as the golden bubbles trickled up the edge of the glass, which she set on a napkin and slid my way across the bar between two regulars. They must be out of coasters, I thought.

I sat alone at a table and watched the Maple Leafs score goal after goal. The dismal delivery of early season hockey coupled perfectly with the uneventful, nondescript, and almost ceremonial undertone of solitude in the depot's whimsically lit and unassuming pub. I wondered what it was, if anything, these men had to be thankful for. Maybe the Maple Leafs winning the Stanley Cup—something they hadn't done for half a century.

The bartender stepped outside, her cigarette already pinched between her chapped red-painted lips, and the door slammed shut, a faded handwritten sign that read "Don't smoke under the roof" in clear view of all the patrons who were also about to do just that.

I finished my beer and looked around the room one last time, putting the empty down on the bar for her to collect on return. The Leafs were up 7–1.

"Not bad for Thanksgiving Monday," I said to the guy right next to me.

"Don't ask me," he shrugged, gesturing to his friend, passed out drunk with his head resting on one open palm. "*He's* the Leafs fan."

I grabbed my bag and boarded the bus. The driver turned off the lights and the blue evening sky of Southern Ontario filled the bus. Passengers became silhouettes as the golden lights of the 401 grew bigger and more beautiful, like Chinese lanterns in the sky, as we left Kitchener. Those silhouetted heads bobbed up and down as the bus bounced, and the bathroom door slammed open and shut along with the rhythmic tumble of the large wheels underneath us. I wondered, for just a moment, if everyone else on this ride was also wondering what the other passengers were thankful for. The Greyhound was silent, the skinny and faded grey dog painted on its side a faithful and loyal companion.

I got out at Dundas and Bay and took a cab north to my apartment on Dupont. The feeling of touching down on the Toronto pavement was like finding sand again after floating well above your height in the ocean: you struggle and bat at the water, and it splashes everywhere. If you're unlucky, you'll be hit with a wave and spun around like a ragdoll, hurtling head over heels. But then you drift to safety, if you just don't fight it. If you let yourself go limp and accept the power that's overtaken you, you'll eventually come back, like a piece of driftwood, to dry land.

I sat down at my kitchen table and opened a can of beer. That red balloon was still in that tree on Yarmouth, trapped in its branches, still desperately trying to break free.

Instead of thinking back to those memories of Murky and Eoin and Walter and Davey and Harrison and Gerry, and their eternal seats in the always-moving van, my mind went ahead to next summer, and I was transported far away from the grey Ontario sky.

I thought of taking the subway down to Union Station and catching a streetcar to the ferry terminal. I thought of standing in line in the blistering sun with my towel around my neck, and my feet in shoes with no socks. I thought of approaching that ticket booth, the cash-only one, and paying for one ferry ticket to Ward's Island. I thought of the jolt forward that big boat would make into the water, of how the skyline of Toronto—so rarely seen from the south—would shrink slightly as I'd float towards the island in that blueish-grey water of Lake Ontario.

The boat would slow as it approached the shore, and with a bump hit its hull against the old rubber tires that line the dock. I'd get out and walk towards the beach. Right before a storm, Lake Ontario has its own waves, too, and despite being incomparable in size and stature to the might of those in the Atlantic, your body nonetheless tumbles around in all of it: the washing machine. With each comforting watery crash, I'd turn and look back towards the sand, at all those people running up and down the beach, becoming smaller by the second, wondering when we'd all be lost forever in the gargantuan pull.

THE FATE OF ALL BANDS

Not just the lifting of amps up countless flights of stairs, sleepless nights, songs and performances gone uncredited, and long cold drives, but also years and years of heartache, desperation, disappointment, and loss: all of these things inspire the sweat that leaves your body every night during a show on tour. Sadness is labour. It's hard work, and it makes you bleed and cry. It builds up a muscle in your heart, and it makes you a great musician.

Heartbreak and torment go headfirst into the writing and performances. Catharsis makes for the most powerful nights, the most tearful, cleansing feelings at its other end. The last chord is the light that's at the end of the day's dark tunnel, and in that sense, writing *is* having your heart broken, and that heartbreak so greatly informs the writing. Every word is a small brick, by which the heart will be repaired.

As the odometer clicked over to half a million kilometres, I sat in the back of the van and thought about all those lovers and friends I'd passed as that big white vehicle lumbered forward on the highway.

I thought of all those people and places I'd encountered along the way, and how we'd left each other behind in our decisions to follow our own signage on the highway. We'd all taken our own exits and ventured off into the horizon to find our own destinations. We sped onward and upward to that beckoning light of the night's stage, as more and more tours came to their end.

I opened and rubbed my eyes, lying down in the back seat. My hangover, a lingering memory of the blurry morning that resided in the back of my head, knocked on my skull like an unwelcome neighbour, my hair dishevelled. My heart beat slowly against my ribs, a dull chime from a clocktower buried in history beneath me.

I looked out the window and realized we'd arrived in the city we were playing that night. The van was stuck, motionless, on a freeway somewhere—Prague? Halifax? Paris? Calgary? Berlin? Ottawa?—and I let out a long yawn, rubbed my eyes again, and sat up.

"Are we here?" I asked the two up front.

"Yeah, man," the driver answered. "Feeling any better?"

"I think so," I responded, buckling up. "Last night . . . Jesus. Holy fuck."

Quickly my hangover was replaced by a deep anticipation. It felt like I'd been to this city before, though maybe I'd only had a glimpse of it. Maybe I only knew it from stories and photographs, or they could be distant memories, perhaps; or maybe I even had the night of my life here once, subliminally craving my return for months or years on end. It's sometimes hard to tell.

The two possibilities went flashing before me: a packed room or an empty room—one or the other. Two sides of a coin. Two colours on the roulette wheel. A great night or a lousy one, those odds are split in half. An excitement brewed inside of me that I couldn't explain to anyone, but as I looked around the van— at the driver, focussed on the traffic ahead, at whoever was in the back next to me, headphones on, completely lost in their thoughts, and at the passenger in the shotgun seat as they looked out the window, the outside world whizzing by—I knew in my ragged heart that everyone had a similar excitement and fear as to what the future held.

On tour, this feeling is repeated daily, at almost exactly three o'clock. The bigger the city, the longer you sit in traffic, and the bigger the look of wonder in your eyes. *What's going to happen to me tonight?* I always thought, every afternoon, around this time. Then we pulled up to the venue, opened the door of the van, and it all began, like it has countless times before, and just like it will again and again and again. *How will the night wrap itself around me like a blanket and escort me off to the dark corners of its world? Will I make new friends tonight? Will I see deep into the heart of this place and its people, be invited in like a native, and see it the way a local would? Or will I leave tomorrow, just as I entered, an outsider, without any stories to tell?*

And then the tour ended: that last show, that last chord. It rang out into the crowd as we exited the stage, grabbed our towels, dried off in the humid chamber of the greenroom.

The next day, the van pulled over to the side of the road, the crunch of gravel like a light rain as the wheels slowed down.

Someone got out of the front seat for one last piss in the tall grass beside the highway. They looked to their left and right, towards the future and the past, and the outside air filled the van with a cleansing reset.

As everyone realized that it was their last-chance piss stop, too, we piled out of the van and, before any time had passed, we were all standing there silently together in the windy grass. I couldn't say for sure, but a part of me felt that everyone might have been thinking the same thing: this might just be the best it's ever going to be.

We climbed back in the van and sped off. I had to come to terms with the fact there was no show tomorrow, and all of a sudden time started to slow down. The present hit me like a brick wall, and that's when I started panicking, thinking of the next tour, looking ahead to starting a new run of shows, repeating the cycle all over again. Repeating this, all over again. All over again. All of the memories from the past few weeks came flooding back to me as everything seemed so incredibly close and yet so very far away.

ACKNOWLEDGEMENTS

Extra special thanks to Maggie Belanger for putting up with me always being away, my mother Wendy for being a non-stop inspiration, my incredible team Dawn Loucks, Sheila Roberts, and Cristina Fernandes for their hard work and dedication, all the amazing staff at ECW for their support over the years and steadfast belief in the writing, and all the people along this seemingly infinite highway across the world for their passion and generosity over the years. Peace and love and rock and roll to all of you.